A THOUSAND PIECES

IAN J. KEENEY

GO FILMINGO
Copyright © 2010 by Ian J. Keeney
First Published: 6/13/2011

ISBN-13: 978-0692250358
ISBN-10: 0692250352

IanJKeeney.com

Cover art by Whitespyder Design
Kristin Holzer (graphic designer/illustrator)
Whitespyder.com

Also available by Ian J. Keeney

A Better Tomorrow

*An award-winning character driven sci-fi action novel about the
movement of consciousness through the multiverse in search of lost love.*

Available in ebook, paperback and audiobook format.

ISBN-10: 1482751410
ISBN-13: 978-1482751413

PROLOGUE

James

Lost in the indescribable indeterminacy all I see is darkness, no lights profoundly finding my way through the mystery. Upon the rickety roof of the attic, rain falls like splinters from the sky, breaking apart the very shelter over my head. Lit only by a flickering orange glow from a half melted candle and the stunning blue flashes of lightning, blinding even the scurrying mouse, I rummage my way through the dusty, dirty old boxes covered in cobwebs.

I remember being a child, staying in this old Victorian home and feeling very scared and alone here. After my grandfather had died, it was just my grandmother and me in this large empty home where nothing but the driving hand of the clock could be heard through the deafening silence. This house has always frightened me and even still as an adult, chills run down my spine just being here.

You may wonder what I'm doing in an old attic with no lights on a dark and stormy night, like I'm almost asking for trouble. I'm not one who believes much in ghosts or the supernatural, but I'm also not one who likes to play the odds. If I'm wrong and there are such beings, I would rather just live my life without knowing. I guess how I live my life is very much like this dark and stormy night: dark and mysterious, yet a glimmer of hope from an overworked candle with bursts of passion every now and again, (like an electric bolt charging through the sky, desperately seeking a place to ground itself) bringing the night back into the darkness, making the creatures of the night less vulnerable and able to hide comfortably within their own shadows.

When I was a child, I grew up in this home. My parents, they were not any part of my life. My mother, unlike my father, was gone by no choice of her own. She passed away shortly after I was born. I didn't get a chance to know her at all. I wasn't even a year old when she died. I don't know how she passed away. It wasn't until much later in my life that I found out she was gone. I guess people have a hard time breaking the news of death and explaining to a child what it is. How do we explain something if we don't even know ourselves? When your grandson asks, "Where's Mommy?" how do you explain, "She's dead." Furthermore, how do you explain to a child what death is? "Where did she go when she died?" How do you explain that? Death is not the end? She's waiting in Heaven? The stork drops you off when you are born, and the tall scary figure in a black cloak that carries a sharp weapon takes you back to where you came from? Where exactly is it that we came from? Too many questions with no answers and that is why I didn't learn until much later in life, my mother was gone for good.

These boxes are filled with old memories. These things I haven't seen since I was a child: toys I used to play with, old photographs, my teddy bear and blanket – the times when life was simple. If only I had known how precious childhood was, I would have enjoyed it a lot more. Most of it was spent alone playing video games while blasting bad music (what I used to think was good), watching movies and doing whatever I wanted. An endless amount of time comes in abundance. When you're a child, you don't realize just how much freedom you really do have. As an adult, we become a prisoner to our own devices. We are bound to a world of responsibilities and race against the clock, fighting our wrinkles against each drive of the second hand, trying our best to keep up. Time grows short as we grow weak and all is lost behind.

My wife and I are separated because we didn't have the time to work out our issues, which brings me to why I'm in this creepy old home on such a night. My grandmother passed away about a year ago. I've been working on this house, fixing it up in my spare time, hoping to sell it for what it should be worth. My wife kicked me out of the house, or I decided to leave, or both – a mutual separation. We just stopped getting along at one point. I'm not exactly sure at what point that was, why we argue so much now, how love turned to hate, but it did. Well, maybe not hate. Not yet anyway, but a lot of anger and tension exists between the two of us.

I packed a big bag and made my way over here in the rain. Perfect weather. Rain. It's very symbolic for the melancholy mood, sadness, depression, anguish, and all the feelings that come from a separation. A lot of people believe that our moods are affected by the weather; however, I once heard that it is the other way around. The collective mood of the people can be so strong that the energy can actually affect the weather. For example, if it's a good time and a lot of shared joy and happiness, the sun will also beat rays of happy sunshine down to the earth. On days where a lot goes wrong and they are filled with a morbid unhappiness, the sun will be just as hard to find as our joy, buried beneath some dark and dismal cloud, lost somewhere in the sky. That makes more sense to me. I'm not unhappy because there is thunder and lightning outside my window. There is thunder and lightning outside my window because I am unhappy, because I got into an argument with my wife. Sometimes I can be happy in the rain or sad on a sunny day.

I'd like to know; when in life does the sadness go away? It seems as though I watch misery rain down around me with an enormous black cloud over my head every single day. It's been raining a lot lately. Is that because there has just been a general, collective unhappiness within everyone these days? Come to think of it, everyone does seem unhappy. There was once upon a time that I was happy, but ever after I am drowning in my misery. My wife had a lot to do with that happiness. So did my daughter. I don't have any of that now. What's left to be happy about?

Often I dream about disappearing to some far off island in paradise – a one way ticket to the middle of nowhere. I think I'd be overwhelmed with joy living out the rest of my life somewhere like Fiji, Bermuda or Bora Bora. Its pure fluorescent blue water as clear as glass as far as the eye can see, barely in motion, astounds me. The rich green islands, the pure fresh air, not a cloud in the sky – it would all be a dream come true. So, what's holding me back? Why am I just hanging out in the attic of my late grandmother's home, away from my wife and daughter? I guess along with the overwhelming excitement of the fantasy island comes also the paralyzing fear of change. It would be completely alien to me, living in paradise. I find it easier to stick with what I know and continue being pedestrian in my own life.

Now I have to figure out what I want. Maybe I want to sit in sorrow in this dark, lonely home and continue being a miserable recluse. Perhaps I should call my wife and apologize, even though I don't think I'm the one who was wrong. My third choice is, I can journey away from it all to some peaceful faraway land and let all my life's worries melt away in the warm tropics with a Bahama Mama (and maybe I'll have a drink too). My choice right now is, I'm going to bed.

CHAPTER | 1

When I was brushing the dust and cobwebs from my childhood memories in the attic of my late grandmother's home, it became apparent to me that my life had not turned out the way I had hoped it would. I've come to realize that life can be either a series of events that just happen to us as we make one reactionary decision after the next, or it can be an array of choices that we make and have to live with. The choices could cause joy or regret, but at least it was a choice. As I reminisced, I became despondent about my life, a combination of a few bad choices and mostly a series of events that happened to me – alone and separated from my wife and child, growing up without my parents, losing my grandmother, displaced from my home and embarking on a frightening new chapter with little hope. As I rummaged through those old memories in heartache, I didn't realize it was about to get worse.

O'Leary's Pub is just a few short steps down the block from grandma's house. As the rain ceased and tiredness had not yet fatigued me, I decided that I needed a drink to help ease my worried mind. I put on my boots and trekked through the slushy sidewalks to get me to the neighborhood bar. The bar has been around since the moment the town was erected. I think the Irishmen poured off the boat in Ellis Island, drove about thirty miles south, saw the beach and hammered the flag into the sand. It has been there ever since and, still to this day, a renovation has never been done once. The pub is dimly lit with old wood paneling on the walls and a gray cement floor. The walls are peppered with memorabilia of a finer day, which symbolizes hope and happiness when this town once must have been alive, or at least this is the place you went to feel alive. Either way, it has an old world sort of charm to it. Although it seems like the biggest hole in the wall, it's the place to be and for some reason carries all of my favorite draught beers. I decided to be a little different that night, though, and in a mental holiday to my paradise island, I downed a few Mai Tais.

Considering it was a Thursday night, it was pretty crowded. It looked as if a band is set up to play on the stage, but I didn't see any musicians around. Maybe the crowd was waiting for the band. I just wanted to drop down a few shots, make myself sleepy and head back home to bed. I couldn't help but notice a girl to my left who was smiling at me the entire time and, though I made eye contact several times, I don't think I've smiled back once. Am I that much of a misanthropic dejected soul that I couldn't even smile back? I just wanted to pay my bill and get out of there.

"Hey, didn't you see me smiling at you?" she said as I turned around, feeling her hand upon my shoulder.

"I'm not wearing my glasses and I'm pretty buzzed," I replied. "Your face was just a blur from that far away."

"So what about now? You see me smiling?"

"Yeah."

She continued and asked me if I would be interested in leaving the bar with her. I was ready to leave anyway so after a slight hesitation of thought, I told her she could join me on my walk around the neighborhood.

It's almost frightening how the little choices we make in life, seemingly insignificant at the time we make them, can lead us into disaster. Who would have known that a smile would lead to a simple walk and that harmless walk could turn into something worse?

I remember riding my bike down the same sidewalk as a kid, playing games with my friends. I wouldn't have predicted in my innocent youth that I would be walking down that same street holding the hand of some big-breasted no-name woman in a leather skirt.

"What are you thinking about?" she asked, breaking the silence.

Not wanting to admit what I was actually thinking, I replied, "Nothing."

"How come you're so quiet?"

"I don't know. What's your name?" I asked, hoping to change the subject.

"Chrystal. You?"

"James."

I was holding her hand because she took it. I didn't make any moves for her. I had hoped she wasn't getting any ideas.

"What's wrong?" she asked.

"Nothing."

"Nobody goes to a bar by themselves and gets drunk if nothing's wrong, unless they're looking for something."

"I'm not looking. My wife and I separated recently."

"Small world," she said. "I'm going through a divorce right now too."

"We're not getting a divorce. We're just separated," I sternly replied.

"You still love her?"

"Yeah. I do. We have a daughter."

"I have a son. It's not easy when kids are involved, but for his sake we're better off apart."

She sat down on a bench under a streetlamp that faced the river. The night was cool, but not unbearable. We sat for a while and talked. It's what I needed, not lying in bed alone, not the comfort of alcohol, I just needed someone to talk to.

"Things had been good before we separated," I told her. "I've never had so much fun in all my life. We did everything together. I don't mean everything as in following each other around like dogs. That wasn't the case at all. We both very much enjoyed our alone time as much as we enjoyed our time together. What I mean is, we did everything. We did the normal things like dinners and movies, but we enjoyed so much more. We went to Broadway musicals, comedy clubs, concerts, casinos, hiking, mountain biking, the beach, traveled all across the globe; and, my wife, she's so beautiful. It's rare to find a woman of such beauty who enjoys all the same things I do, even camping. I've dated a lot of women in my younger days that wouldn't go anywhere near the woods, never mind hike trails or deal with the bugs by the lake. Hiking in heels would be really quite difficult and the perfume, that's surely going to attract a swarm of bugs. She is different though. She can be beautiful in a dress, all done up with elegance and class, but can also put on a pair of work boots and jeans without being afraid of getting dirty."

"I can tell you really love her," she said as she turned her head from the water to look at me.

"I remember a time when we climbed a tree together and sat up on a branch, looking out over the lake at sunset. The golden sun glistened across the lake with glitter in the waves as we held each other up in the tree, inspired by the beauty. I was happy then. Sometimes I would be driving home from work and just the thought of her in my life would bring an enormous smile to my face. She always made me smile."

"You can make those memories with someone new, if it came to that. I mean, I hope things work out for you and your wife, but what I mean is, don't get so hung up on it. Things will work out for you no matter what."

I know she was right, but I didn't tell her that. I knew even if things didn't work out, I'll be happy in the long run. I didn't expect to fall in love with my wife when I did. I never expected to meet her and never expected to be friends. Now that we're separated, I don't know what to expect next.

I remember the day I fell in love with her. It just hit me. We were friends for a while but there was one particular day when I had a revelation and said to myself, *I love her.* It was a day where everything that could have gone wrong did. I was in the worst of moods, wishing to wallow in my pajama clad misery on the surface of my cloud-like bed, nestled comfortably under my blanket, secured from the world and all its torment. As down as I felt, as sad and angry as I was, to this day I cannot remember why. All I remember is the way I felt the second I saw her face and the big smile that broke through my frown as my teeth sparkled in the sunlight. All I remember is the joy that she made me feel. That was the day when I realized that I was in love.

CHAPTER | 2

A lot of people spend a lot of time and effort searching for love, but if there is anything I've learned about love, it's this: Love finds you.

I've also learned, or so I think, that we can fool ourselves and convince our hearts that we are in love, not because we are but because we want to be. We love the idea of love, being in love, loving someone and someone loving us in return. What a beautiful thing, but it's so hard to find. Sometimes I think we just love the one we're with, not because we love them, but because we want to love. What is love? Is there any true way to define it? I'd like to believe that Kelly and I are in love.

We are perfect for each other, or were perfect, or are; I'm not sure anymore, but we are as close to perfect as we could be, or could have been. Kelly has always been a woman of such exquisite beauty – her hair so thick and smooth, perfectly blonde, not too long, not too short and always styled to perfection. She is just the right height for me, a few inches shorter but never taller than me, even in heels, but never too short either, a perfect arms height to wrap her into me and lock together as a completed puzzle when we hug. It is as though our bodies were made for each other and I believe the same, too, applies for our souls as if perhaps, should such thing exist, we are soul mates. Her body is the definition of perfection, something so perfect I could never believe she was real, but she is. I must have been dreaming, having a girl like that in my life and able to call her my own.

The funny thing is, though I say she is like a dream come true, she is quite the opposite of whom I pictured myself to end up with. Physically, I was always more interested in darker features in a woman, somewhat of an edge and a bit mysterious – tattoos, piercings and funky hair, someone who could front a rock band is what I was usually attracted to. Kelly is nothing like that at all. She doesn't wear black, she wears bright colors. She doesn't like horror movies, she likes romantic comedies. She doesn't have tattoos, she has baseball jerseys. Love will make you throw your wishlist out the window. When you have love, that is all you need. You can make a list of the picture-perfect man or woman of your dreams: dark hair, blue eyes, smart, funny, sexy, talented, smells nice, clean, and so on; however, there is one thing missing from that list – love; and, once love is on that list you might as well scratch off all the other details, because love is the only thing that matters.

In sickness and in health, in good times and in bad, through all the smiles and the tears, the laughter and the pain, you never for a minute cease to love each other. Then does blonde hair instead of black, or brown eyes instead of blue really matter? No. There is nothing wrong with blonde hair or brown eyes. Kelly's eyes are in fact green, but bear with me. I'm just trying to prove a point.

We got married six years after we first met. I met her at the fireworks on the 4th of July. My heart stopped the moment I saw her and it was her kiss that revived me. She was a friend of a friend, someone with whom I used to work with. Kelly worked with us too, but since it is such a big place, we never met. I knew of Kelly and that she worked with us. Everybody knew Kelly, but she didn't know me. Not then.

My friend who asked me to come along with her and her friends had intentions of me falling for her other friend, Mae. Mae was very pretty, but

Kelly had a personality like I've never seen. She was fun, outgoing, playful, funny but never over the top or obnoxious. She was sweet – a perfect balance. I was so drawn to her. Eventually, from that day, we started bumping into each other more often at work and even ended up working together on the same assignments for a while. One thing slowly led to another from co-workers to friends, friendship to dates then dating to lovers.

We had our ups and downs, like all relationships, but unlike any I've ever had, it was up more than it was down. Life was a party; found on a high from life that we assumed we'd never come down from, we ventured toward the rising sun of the dawn of our relationship. We were inseparable. We had met our final destinations in the search for love. Moment by moment, our love grew stronger and more powerful and one day it just exploded out of us as the fireworks on the day in which we met. Nothing could stop us. Nothing could get in the way of our love.

I proposed to her six years after the day we met, on a cruise ship as we sailed smoothly across the Caribbean during sunset. It was perfect and, of course, she said yes. I have to say, I was very nervous. Sure, we talked about marriage but she had no idea I had a ring and was planning it. I knew she loved me. I was just afraid she was going to say it wasn't the right time. Yeah, after six years. We took our time and there's nothing wrong with that. I wouldn't have had it any other way, nor would she. We have both rushed into big mistakes in the past and we were not about to make one between us. We wanted it to work. Look at us now, though. We still ended up separated, so I don't know if it really made a big difference. I'm sure it did. You can't build a roof without a foundation. The roof just needs a renovation now.

So, after we built our foundation, we answered the ad for the, "contemporary bay front masterpiece, cul-de-sac location, amenities abound. Five bedroom, three and a half bath, living, dining and sun rooms with wet bar, fireplace, gourmet kitchen with huge center island with marble countertops and backsplash. Huge windows and three balconies and a gazebo overlooking the bay. Six zone heat, three zone central air. Two master suits. Pavers and private, maintenance free, fenced in yard for all your toys. New windows and garage doors. This one is a must see!" So, we saw it, and we bought it.

It was a very surreal time in my life. I never thought much about marriage. It seemed like an eternity away, but there I was getting married, vacationing on my honeymoon and buying a house. It didn't seem like it was ever going to happen, but it did.

We weren't even in the house for a year and we added our own little amenity. His name is Daredevil. He was a puppy when we got him but now he's a 6-year-old Doberman Pinscher. He brought a lot of joy to our family. I had a wife, a house, a dog – the job was almost complete. In one week from now, it will be exactly five years ago that our daughter, Alyssa, was born. March 1st.

I didn't know what to expect, being a father. I thought I was going to grow up to be a single man, alone in a dimly lit apartment eating cheap frozen dinners, watching reruns on TV and just wasting my life away. That looks to be the way things may end up after all if this separation does not end in reconciliation. Regardless, I never saw myself as being a husband or a father – especially a father. I didn't care much for kids. They're rambunctious, sticky, smelly, exhausting and a whole lot of responsibility; but, for some reason, after we married, just me, Kelly and Daredevil in that big house with four spare bedrooms, it just seemed right. I changed my mind, and yes, Alyssa has been rambunctious, sticky, smelly, exhausting and a whole lot of responsibility, but I have to say one thing: she is worth every bit of it.

Before Kelly and I were married, neither one of us wanted children. We talked about it a few times. I had my superficial reasons and she had hers. Like I said, she is a picture perfect beauty and she was afraid of losing that figure after having a kid. I guess that's a vain reason to not have a child, but we had other reasons too, such as time, our careers, and our one-on-one relationship. I understand that as soon as a wife becomes a mother, the husband immediately drops a rank on the totem pole.

❖

I stumbled into grandma's house with the girl from O'Leary's Pub as the early birds began waking up. We spent about an hour sitting on the bench by the water, talking about our troubles in love. It's something I'm not used to doing. I asked her how she intended to get home and she said her car was at the pub. I could tell she was still a little tipsy from too many Long Island Iced Teas. I knew she shouldn't drive. I told her she could stay the night, but I let her know how I felt. I didn't want anything physical to happen between us. I could tell her interest was growing, but even if it wasn't, I felt like it was something that had to be said. That's something I've learned as I got older. Sometimes you just have to be blunt in order to avoid becoming embroiled in a bad situation that you never wanted part of.

Although Kelly and I have had our problems, I am still married and even though we are separated, sex with another would be adultery. I don't go to church every Sunday, and I am not the perfect Catholic, but I usually know right from wrong. She respected that. She went into the room downstairs, closed the door and I climbed the steps to my room.

I lied down in my bed trying to get some sleep once and for all, but the morning sun rose and penetrated through my curtains. Meanwhile, my drunkenness slowly turned away into a sober state. I began to accept that I wasn't going to sleep. A rummaging sound from downstairs echoed its way through the empty halls and into my bedroom. I guess Chrystal couldn't sleep either. I thought she was leaving. I wondered if I should say goodbye or just let her sneak out, then decided to get up and make my way out of bed. I traveled to the doorway while rubbing the fatigue out of my eyes. As I descended the staircase, I quickly realized that the girl was rummaging through my refrigerator, wearing nothing but the skin that God gave her. Just as I was thinking she wasn't going to try anything, there she was in my kitchen wearing nothing.

"You know I can see you there," she called out.

"You realize you're naked in my kitchen?"

"I didn't know you were awake."

"Is this really happening right now?"

"I just wanted a snack. You don't mind, do you?"

"That you are naked or that you're having a snack?" I asked.

I knew that she was persistent because of how many times she smiled at me in the bar and then how she came to greet me before I left, but I didn't think she would be this persistent. What was she was trying to do? She wanted me to see her. She wasn't embarrassed at all. I've been with girls like this before. They don't believe a guy when he says no, or they just don't accept it and will do anything it takes to get their way. Some women are masters of manipulation.

"I think it's probably best that you leave," I said.

"Seriously?"

"Yeah, seriously."

She couldn't believe I was turning her down. Truth is, I didn't want to. It wasn't easy. I knew I couldn't go down the steps or that would be it. I would give in and face the rest of my time filled with regret. If I had any hope of working things out with Kelly, I had to stay on those steps. I couldn't go down into temptation. I guess I put myself into these situations sometimes by caring too much or being too nice, but I really didn't feel right sending her back to her car drunk. Maybe that's what I get for allowing a stranger into my home.

A sudden knock hit hard on the door. The doorbell isn't something I got around to fixing yet. She knew her game was over and she hurried back to the bedroom. My lustful eyes watched her run back into the room as my mind thought for a moment of how nice it would have been. I quickly made my way down the stairs and peeked out the window. Kelly's car was in the driveway. Already seeing everything there was to see, I opened the bedroom door and spotted her dressing.

"It's my wife," I said. "I need you to go."

"Okay. I'm sorry. I really didn't want to cause trouble."

Another knock hit the door hard.

"Just stay in here. Lock the door. Be quiet and I'll come get you when it's safe."

I closed the bedroom door behind me and hurried to the front door. I took a breath and opened it.

"Kelly!" I said with a smile.

Kelly stood on the porch with Alyssa and her Hello Kitty backpack. This meant only one thing. Kelly was dropping Alyssa off to stay with me, possibly all night. Ordinarily, I would be really excited about spending the day with my little pumpkin and having a sleep over, but I still hadn't slept. Not only that, there's a naked woman in my house, grandma's house, and – how do I get myself into these crazy situations all the time? I thought this would have ended when I hit thirty. I'm not even trying. Crazy situations just happen to find me, wherever I am. Apparently, it wasn't just a phase. It must be me.

"You've come to take me back?" I said jokingly.

"I need you to take Alyssa for the day," Kelly said as she invited herself into the house.

"Hot date?"

"As a matter of fact, yes."

"You're kidding, right? I thought we just separated, taking some time alone. Ya know, alone."

"Not in front of Alyssa."

A sudden crash from Grandpa's bedroom alerted both of us to draw our attention to the closed door.

"What was that?" Kelly asked.

"I don't know."

"Someone's here?"

"The cat."

"You got a cat?" she asked with suspicion.

"Yeah."

"When did you get a cat?"

"Forget the cat. What's this about a date?"

"I was just saying it to make you jealous. I have to work late."

This is in part why we separated. My jealousy, feasibly, but she has given me plenty of reasons to be jealous. I know we are separated. Maybe I'm just too much of a dreamer, thinking that we will work everything out and get back together. If I had known Kelly was going to bring Alyssa over, I never would have let Chrystal stay the night. These are the complications of being separated. I never intended to sleep with her. She was drunk and I could not let her go back to the bar and drive home. I assume I could have called her a cab, but I didn't see any harm in letting her stay in the spare room. It is the battle of who is right and who is wrong.

Kelly left Alyssa with me and the cat, also known as Chrystal. I guess she believed the cat story at the time. Either that or she had no choice but to believe it. She had to go to work. Usually her mother, Paige, watches Alyssa while she's at work, but Paige couldn't watch her that day. She dropped her off with me instead.

I plopped Alyssa in front of the TV immediately. I normally wouldn't do that. I would usually take her to the park. Having a kid is a great excuse to run around on the jungle gym as an adult without getting any unusual looks. It would look strange if I, a grown man, showed up to the park all by myself to go down the slide and swing on the swing set.

I went back to check on Chrystal while Alyssa was engrossed in her cartoons. She was dressed, sitting on the bed and waiting for me. I peeked out the window to make sure Kelly had gone.

"I'm going to take Alyssa into the kitchen to fix her a snack," I said. "When we're in there, just quickly and quietly sneak out the front door."

"I'm sorry. I didn't mean to cause you any trouble."

"You didn't, but it was too close. Don't worry about it, but you have to go."

"Okay. I had a nice night."

"Me too."

I genuinely did have a good night, talking with her and opening up to her. It's something I don't get to do often enough.

"Good luck," she added as I was leaving the room.

"Thanks."

I closed the door behind me, and took Alyssa away from the cartoons to make her an apple with peanut butter.

❖

After I made the peanut butter and apple for Alyssa, I brewed myself a pot of coffee – a whole pot. By the time she was done eating, the coffee was ready. She didn't finish the apple, but she was finished eating. I poured the coffee into a Thermos, grabbed a travel mug and took her to Jenkinson's Boardwalk. I didn't want to just keep her in the house all day. It's not her fault that I didn't sleep. With limited time together because of the separation, I had to make the most of it for her. I didn't want her childhood to be like mine. It wasn't very fulfilling because my grandparents were old when they raised me. They did the best they could. I want to do the best I can for Alyssa. I figured I could put her on a few rides, give her some coins for the arcade and she could occupy herself as I sipped my coffee to stay awake.

As we walked up the ramp to the boardwalk, we passed by pirate themed mini-golf. She grabbed a cannon that was leaning on the ground and lifted it up.

"Dad! Dad! Look how strong I am!"

"That's great sweetie."

I didn't have the heart to tell her that it wasn't a real bronze cannon, but just a painted foam replica.

"Can we play?"

"Don't you want to go on the rides?"

"I wanna play."

"Can we go on some rides first and play later? What rides do you want to go on?"

"The dragon!"

"Okay. Let's go on the dragon first and we'll come back."

The dragon is a ride like the teacups. They go in a circle and the riders sit inside the dragon and can spin the dragon around. I knew I would have to go on this with her. She wouldn't let me stand by and watch, but at least I could sit.

After the dragons, I put her on all the standard rides: the motorcycles that go in a circle and scream, "bizz, bizz, bizz, bizz," giving me a splitting headache, boats that went in a circle, balloons that went in a circle, elephants that went in a circle, trucks that went in a circle, the carousel that went in a circle and a school bus that goes up and down.

By the time we finished with the rides, she was pretty exhausted too. Not only did she forget about the mini-golf, she also lost interest in going to the arcade. Going in circles for too long can tire anyone out. I could tell she was exhausted so I took her back to the car without even telling her that we were leaving. She didn't object when she saw the car.

Once we got back from the boardwalk, I was exhausted despite all the coffee I drank. I fell asleep on the couch with Alyssa as we watched television, waiting for Kelly to pick her up. Kelly came to pick her up and didn't say a word to me, not even thank you. She only spoke to Alyssa. I

don't know if she did it on purpose or not, but it
hurt me either way. Our feelings really had grown
apart. There used to be a time when I wouldn't
even look at another woman, but even if I did, there
were no bad thoughts and I would never give a
second glance. Even though I'm hurting, I noticed
how attractive Chrystal was. That stood out to me
because it was the first time I ever saw someone as
that attractive other than my wife. I guess once
someone hurts you enough, you just stop caring so
much. The thing is, no matter how much Kelly
hurts me, I will never stop loving her. That may be
a flaw, if one can be too forgiving or love too much.
Most people, they wouldn't want to get back
together with her. They'd be finding some way to
get revenge. Yet, though Kelly is far from flawless,
she has a way of turning everything around to be
my fault.

   She has never cheated on me, or so she
claims, but I have always had a sense of something
mysterious. Her phone is always ringing off the
hook from guys I don't know. She never stops
texting. We would be out to dinner and she'd be
sitting there at the table texting another man.
Whether they were sleeping together or not became
irrelevant to me. I thought she was inconsiderate,
disrespectful and rude. She thought I was overly
controlling. Again, it is the battle between who is
right and who is wrong.

   There were days when she would disappear. I
couldn't reach her. She'd be on the road for work
and she would just vanish, not answer her calls,

texts or emails. No one knew where she was. Then she would arrive home with some excuse as to why I couldn't reach her and why she couldn't call me. She dropped her cell phone in the sink full of water and it stopped working. She couldn't get an Internet connection. She didn't have change for a payphone and didn't think to call collect. She thought it was okay to leave me hanging for days on end, not knowing how my wife was doing. Maybe what she said was the truth, just as Chrystal was just some random woman from the bar that slept in that room alone and nothing more. From the outside looking in, it appears to be monstrous fabrications and mistruths to portray an image of innocence. It all seems so unrealistic. I'm sure she knew I don't really have a cat.

Maybe it was all the truth and she's right. Maybe I am controlling with jealousy problems and now I'm getting a taste of my own poison. I just think she has to be more understanding of my feelings. If my wife doesn't come home until 2 am, I want to know where she is. I don't think that is controlling. I am just concerned.

What upsets me more than anything about this is that Alyssa is being dragged through it all. I just want her to lead a normal life and that's been so hard for her thus far.

CHAPTER | 3

Kelly

IT'S been raining for days, raining more than what seems to be normal. Nothing seems to be normal anymore. I put so much blame on my husband for what happened with our separation, but most of all I am angry for Alyssa. I'll be okay. I'm worried about her. She needs a man in her life that can be a real father, a role model. He used to be, but things have changed. He changed. The fast pace of life with the drama of working on both our ends caused him to fold under pressure. He became distant, argumentative and sometimes downright mean. I've been placing all the blame on him but, honestly, I think that is my way of folding under the pressure, too. We are all far from perfect, I know. I'm no exception. I've become distant, too busy and not there for him as much as he needed me when he needed me the most. I focused on more selfish things, my career to be exact. We both have high demanding careers, and that takes a lot away from our relationship sometimes. It never became this big of a problem until now though.

We both work together, which is how we met. Officially, we met though my friend at the 4th of July fireworks, but it was at work where we started to get to know each other. I'm an investigative journalist with my own national TV show. He's a cameraman at the station. We began working together often and slowly got to know each other. I never mixed business with pleasure and neither did he. The thing is, we were so infatuated that we decided to break our rule. I'll never forget the first time I saw him. He looked me right in the eyes, smiled a big beautiful smile and waved to me. I couldn't help but smile back. That's not normal for me. I usually keep my guard up or I am just flat-out uninterested, but he captivated me from the moment I saw him. It made no sense to me that I had such feelings for someone who was basically a stranger. I didn't know what it was. I've never felt that before and I've never felt it since. It usually takes me several meetings for me to remember someone's name, but I remembered James and never forgot it. I said his name in my daydreams many times.

We both had these feelings from the moment we met and I think we both kind of knew it, but since we work together, it took a long time before those feelings developed into something. We had a great relationship built on friendship, but it became effortful after awhile to uphold both a professional and personal relationship together. We never had our privacy.

We decided we had to do something about that or the relationship would end up falling apart. He asked his supervisor to be transferred to work in the studio, rather than in the field. Most of my work was in the field. That's when things were the best for us, when we made that change. We never saw each other at work anymore but after work, we could go out and enjoy being a couple. That was the time in our lives when he proposed to me. We got married, bought a house together, one we could start a family in, and, we did.

It wasn't until recently, maybe about six months ago, that I was traveling and doing a lot of shows on the road. I left for days at a time. We both work in the New York City, but we are not city people. He was born and raised in Matawan, New Jersey and I grew up in West Des Moines, Iowa. Though I love the experience of the big city, I still appreciate coming home to a more relaxing environment. I need a balance, one of the many things we have in common. We enjoyed our home on the bay in Atlantic Highlands. The problem is, I was barely home anymore. It was a very strenuous life for him when I was away. He had to work, take care of Alyssa, watch after Daredevil, keep up the house, pay the bills; the list goes on. He did everything while I was away. He was stretched too thin and really losing his mind, I think. He would get stressed, and I knew he was upset with me. More often than not, I would only be home one day out of the week. He was very argumentative over the phone, so I would just stop calling him when I was away. I could not stand the fighting. I would just make excuses that my phone broke so we wouldn't have to talk.

When I arrived home, he was always distant with me. He knew that we had enough money for me to stay at home, but I didn't struggle my entire life to make it this far and become a stay-at-home mom. I had dreams. I am living them now. I'm on TV with my own show. It doesn't get better than that. It's what I always wanted so it's not so easy to just let blow away in the wind like dandelion spores. It's unreasonable for him to think I'd give that all up. I cannot give that up. Not so soon. He thought family should come first. It's not like family isn't important to me. He just didn't understand. He still doesn't. I'm sure if I quit my job everything would be fine, for him.

I'm glad for the things I do have, the simple pleasures that I'm allowed because of my hard work, like my nice car to keep us safe while driving home in the rain, or the garage to keep us dry when going into our modern home. I count my blessings every day. I really do. I never take any of it for granted. Not everyone is so fortunate. I know some people don't even have a home, and, right now as I stand in my garage holding my daughter in my arms, gazing out at the heavy rain pouring down like a tropical storm, I know there's a mother and daughter holding tight for warmth, seeking temporary shelter from the downpour.

I care. I pray. That's all I know how to do. I wish there were something more I could do to help them, but I don't know what it is. That's the story of my life, always wanting to do good but never knowing how. As a result, I do nothing. I'll make lunch for Alyssa whilst knowing other children are starving on the weekends because all they eat is one meal a day during the week: school lunch with a meal ticket.

It must be difficult for those less fortunate children. Alyssa hasn't had it easy either in her short life. I know how hard it must be for their parents. As a mother, I know, all you want is for your child to be healthy and happy, living a better life than you did as a child. Alyssa always had the luxury of all the best that materialism has to offer, but no matter how hard you prepare to give your child a good life, you can't really prepare for them to get sick.

It's probably the most frightening thing a parent can go through, not knowing what is wrong with your child. Doctor after doctor and test after test, we found out she had a very rare form of leukemia. It wasn't until we took her to the children's hospital in Philadelphia that she was diagnosed and able to get the treatment that she needed.

She went through everything from stem cell transplantation to blood and platelet transfusions and a bone marrow transfusion. I wanted to do everything I could for her. I wanted to donate my bone marrow for her transfusion, but I wasn't a match. Her father was and, as weird as it sounds, that upset me. It's better him than any random stranger, but I wanted it to be me. I was so scared for her. I cried every single night, asking God why He was putting her through this. It didn't make any sense to me. She is just a child. I really lost my faith then. I used to believe in God, but I've had a hard time believing in a God who would put people through such horrific things, especially a child. James told me that the reason God puts us through such struggles is not to punish us but to make us stronger. We learn and build strength and courage through struggle. He believes that going through something like that makes us all stronger, her, him and me. Should this happen again, his belief is that, though it will still be tough, having gone through such a trial once, we can be stronger the next time life throws us a surprise. I'm not sure if I believe that yet. Some will say that it's through the Grace of God and others will attribute it to the advances of medical science, but however it happened, Alyssa is fine now. She has all the energy any little 4-year-old could possibly have. I know this separation must be hard on her, though.

I said I wasn't going to sit around and do nothing anymore. Perhaps I should apply that to my own life, too. I'm going to call him, for her, for us, and try to work it out. I know it's the right thing to do. We were happy once. We were once madly in love. We still are in love, I suppose. You don't just stop loving someone, do you? It's just that other stuff piles up on top of that feeling, making it hard to know that it's there. Perhaps it's time to pack away my pride and all those other feelings and focus on what's most important: Love. I would never have done that before. I know I'm always right, to a flaw. Maybe he's right. Maybe I have grown stronger through my trials. I am a stronger person now.

CHAPTER | 4

James

THE pieces of our marriage have been broken and spread about like a jigsaw puzzle on the table, waiting to be put together again. As we sat there in the same restaurant that we visited on our first official date, it's a bit mysterious as though we aged twelve years but we haven't moved an inch. We sat, trying to put the puzzle together, but we know what happens. You put a puzzle in the closet and don't touch it for years. When you want to put it together, the box says it's supposed to have a thousand pieces. Nobody counts to make sure all those pieces are in the box before they start constructing the little cardboard shapes into a bigger picture. You build the puzzle, and when you get as far as you can go, you realize there are holes in that big picture, and it's not exactly what you thought it would be. There are missing pieces. Nobody knows where they went. They're just gone. You look in the box. They're not there. You look under the table. They're not there either. You just have an incomplete picture. It's not bad, but it's not everything you thought it would be. I'm afraid that's how Kelly had become, like that old dusty puzzle, a potentially beautiful picture missing a lot of pieces.

I didn't know what her intentions were. It's not like her to call on me unexpectedly. She's usually very stubborn. It was very unusual for her to call me up and request a dinner. It remained a mystery while our mouths moved more for chewing than talking. Have we become that used to each other, or have we become that distant? I'd say maybe uninterested, but I'm not. I am still interested in her and she must be interested in me or why else would she have called to have dinner? When we were there on our first date, it was altogether different. We had fun. We laughed at each other's free, nonsensical behavior. We gazed into each other's ravenous eyes with passion. This time we didn't even make eye contact. The most important thing I said was, "Can you pass the salt, please?" It felt like I've had a more thorough conversation with the waiter than I had with my wife. It felt as though there was a cold wall, she and I divided by a glacier, twenty feet of frigid blue ice between her and me.

Looking back on that night, as boring and as uneventful of a meal that it started out to be, as forgetful as it was – it was a night that I will never forget. When you think you've been through it all, seen the worst of it, life reminds you that everything is a gamble and you've just rolled snake eyes.

Kelly had left Alyssa with her sole surviving grandparent that night, Kelly's mother, Paige. She was always good at watching Alyssa for us. It was always a pleasure for her. Widowed and alone, Alyssa was welcomed company for Paige. That night was different though. Paige called Kelly during dinner. The phone rang and the ID said, "Home," so we knew it was about Alyssa. Why else would she call at dinner? At first you think, Alyssa needs something. Maybe we need to pick up some milk on the way home. Maybe she's being bad or not feeling well. I wasn't sure, but when I saw the look on Kelly's face the moment she said, "Hello," I knew it was much worse. This wasn't about milk or an upset stomach. This was a big deal and, given her medical history, I thought the worse.

Kelly's face suddenly turned into a panic. She got up and grabbed her things, exclaiming, "We have to go! Right now! We have to go home!"

For no reason would I have ever expected to hear what I heard when Kelly put the phone to my ear. I heard Paige screaming. I heard my mother-in-law shouting for help and a world of chaotic banging and scuffling in the background. I called out for Paige but it was in vain. I don't think she had the phone to her ear.

Without hesitation, I grabbed my phone from my pocket and dialed 9-1-1, not wanting to disconnect the call on Kelly's phone. I alerted the police and then ran out of the restaurant to our car right away. I didn't even realize at the time that we were skipping out on the bill, but I went back to the restaurant a few days later to explain what happened and pay for the meals. I was shocked when they told us not to pay after I told them what happened. I insisted but they waved my money away. They had read in the newspaper what happened, so they knew I wasn't making up stories to save money on a meal.

I drove home that night like lightning, faster than I had ever driven before. Even still, the police were there first and the perpetrator was already gone; and, so was my daughter. I feel bad for the officer whose job it was to not only explain to Kelly and me that both Alyssa and Paige were gone, but that we couldn't go inside because our home was a crime scene. They asked us a lot of difficult questions, none of which I can remember. They were trying to understand what happened and gain any insights into who may have taken Alyssa and Paige and killed our dog, Daredevil, but I don't think we were of any help. We were in complete shock. That night is still a fog to me, like a dream when you wake up and are struggling to remember bits and pieces; flashing lights, curious neighbors, and where were those neighbors when we needed them? They didn't hear anything, or were they too afraid to care? The police had but one fragment of evidence to go on, a muddy footprint left behind on our carpet from a work boot. With that, they promised to do everything they could to find Alyssa and Paige and bring justice upon the man who infiltrated our lives.

Since our home was considered a crime scene, they wouldn't let Kelly go inside for her things, not even a change of clothes or her toothbrush. I don't see why taking a toothbrush from the home would have upset the investigation, but that's how it was. We couldn't go inside while they were still investigating. I guess they didn't want us to walk around the house while they were still searching for evidence. One female officer was nice enough to sneak down a few clothing items for Kelly, then we stopped off at a drug store and bought whatever else she needed. It was the middle of the night, searching in the cold and dilapidated twenty-four-hour drug store, lit in pale green lighting. It felt like the type of place that you would see on the news, the corner store that got robbed. The place seemed like the perfect target. I guess my mind was going and I was overly shaken-up from what we were going through. I just wanted her to get a toothbrush, shampoo and whatever else she needed and get out of there.

We stayed with each other that night at my late grandmother's Victorian home, the place I have been staying lately. She could have gotten a hotel room, but I didn't feel comfortable with her being alone that night. I don't think she did either. I know we were supposed to be separated, but things change overnight. We couldn't be alone.

Neither one of us was able to sleep. We were on the couch. She laid with her head against my chest while I held her tight in my arms while she cried through the night. I sat with a stern grimace, filled with mixed emotions. Anguish corroded my heart while a stronger emotion, animosity, poisoned my soul. I was starving for revenge, but I knew I was right where I was supposed to be, with Kelly. I could've driven around like a lunatic chasing ghosts but it would have done us no good. The police are doing their job. There wasn't much for me to do. That is where I needed to be, with my wife.

It's ironic, of all the stories that Kelly and I reported throughout our careers, we never thought that we'd someday become a story. I know how it feels, your privacy lost for the freedom of strangers to gossip about you or maybe feel better about themselves because their life isn't as bad. Whatever the reason, I didn't like it. Not if it wasn't going to help bring Alyssa home. It was all over the news that night, the daughter of a famous TV news journalist kidnapped.

It was for that reason the police were almost certain that this was not a random kidnapping. They first started digging through all of Kelly's stories, starting with the most recent and working backward, trying to find any leads they could, any potential suspects. As they were going through hours upon hours of file footage and old contacts, the first lead came to us on our doorstep.

Once the sun arose on the morning after Alyssa was taken, I went out to see what the newspapers were saying about our case. As soon as I opened the door, I noticed something very strange. On the front steps was a puzzle box and attached to it, a note. I looked at it for a good long time. I knew it was in relation to Alyssa but I didn't know why, and I was frightened. I didn't want to read the letter or see what was in the box. This startled me, not only for Alyssa but for Kelly and myself as well. In addition to finding Alyssa at home, he knew he could find us at my grandmother's house. He obviously knew a lot more about us then we did about him, and if he knows where we are, he must be watching us.

I pulled the handwritten letter off of the box from the one piece of tape that was holding it down. It read, "No police. You are being watched." That's all that was written.

I didn't really think about it. I didn't feel threatened, but I didn't dismiss it either. I didn't know what to think. I put the letter into my pocket and brought the puzzle inside. I wasn't sure if I should let Kelly see it or not, but I knew she would be upset if I kept something like that a secret from her. I didn't know what the puzzle was and, if it was something bad, I was afraid of her being upset even more than she was already.

I didn't like feeling as though I had no control. I was supposed to be the protector of the family. If that's the case, I failed miserably. With careful consideration, I came to the conclusion that I should not keep the jigsaw puzzle a secret from her. We emptied the pieces onto the table together. A thousand pieces of cardboard spilled over the edge and hit the wooden table like rain. We began putting it together piece by piece. It was quite a difficult puzzle. Most of it was hundreds of tiny black pieces and we had no frame of reference. It was clearly obvious, even before the moment all the pieces spilled from the box and onto the table, that this puzzle was not the picturesque waterfall scene illustrated on the front. This was something different, more cynical and perhaps a clue from the man who took Alyssa.

As we put the puzzle together, we realized that all the black pieces were the darkness of a dimly lit room. In the middle, we were beginning to see that, amongst all the obscurity, there was a figure – the outline of a person. The more pieces we put together, the more we were realizing, this figure in the picture was Alyssa.

We put the entire puzzle together and, before our eyes was a horror to behold: a photograph of our child sitting in a wooden chair within the depths of darkness. It took us several minutes to see through our tears and realize that the puzzle was incomplete. Neither one of us had any pieces left, but there was a hole in the picture. Something was missing. We looked briefly for the missing pieces by lifting up the box and looking on the floor around us, but it only took a moment to realize that those pieces were purposely excluded from the box.

Looking just close enough to the puzzle we could see within this shadowy room, all dressed in black, a figure stood behind Alyssa. The pieces that were missing, just a few, were enough so the face of this figure would be absent from the big picture, thus our puzzle was incomplete. The biggest question I had was, why would he send us a puzzle? What was the point of us putting together a complicated puzzle to see a picture of Alyssa? Was he trying to torment us? He didn't give us any demands. He didn't ask for a ransom. He just gave us a puzzle. Then the biggest question arose. I did not inform Kelly of the letter that was taped to the box. Unknowing of the letter, she suggested that we should call the police and show them the puzzle. I pulled the letter out of my pocket and handed it to her. She looked at it and read it to herself, "No police. You are being watched," but she spoke no words.

After a moment's thought, I took the letter from her and said, "I have an idea."

I took a picture of the puzzle with my digital camera and made a printout. I wrote a note that asked that all police contact with us be handled circumspectly. I put my letter and the photograph in an envelope, along with the handwritten note from the kidnapper, and addressed it to Detective Kercher, the one in charge of our case. I took it to the post office with a few other things mixed in. The reason I brought it to the post office was so he wouldn't go through my mailbox and see the letter addressed to the police. I carried it with other mail so it didn't seem as if I was going out of my way to deliver one suspicious letter. It was scary to me that he was tracking my every move. What made me more fearful was it made me think that he was also following every move that Kelly made as well. He must have been following us for a while.

When I got out of the post office, I saw there was another note, this time on the windshield of my car. I walked up to the car and looked at the note flapping in the frigid breeze, then looked around. I didn't look at the note. I knew he had to be close by. I quickly made my way to the corner of the building, all the way around the back, up the side and into the parking lot again – a full circle around the building. There was no one. Whoever put that letter on my windshield left quickly and without a trace.

I approached my car and pulled the letter out from under the windshield wiper. I unfolded it. It was nothing more than a phone number on a piece of paper. I got into the car, took out my cell phone and dialed the number. There was no ring. It went directly to a pre-recorded message of a man who spoke with a very subtle accent that I didn't quite recognize. Perhaps Russian or Greek. Maybe even a southern accent. Like I said, it was subtle. He may have even made it up to disguise his voice. I'm not too familiar with accents. The only thing I could be sure of is that he wasn't from around here. He had a deep voice and was rather soft spoken.

"By now you know that I have your daughter and your wife's old mother. I will tell you where to find them, though I suppose you are more concerned with your daughter. She will be unharmed if you carefully follow my instructions. For each job well done, your daughter will be one step closer to you. You were instructed not to communicate with the police. If I find you cooperating with the police from this moment forth, there will be consequences suffered. Your wife's mother, I do not need her and her loss can be upon your head. As a sign of good faith, the first job will be an easy one. Do all the jobs properly and no one will be hurt. Here is your first job. Listen carefully. You can only hear this message once. It will be erased. Withdraw the sum of ten thousand dollars from your bank account. Not your wife's. Not your joint account. It must be your account and she is not to know. Put the money in a bag and make sure it is secured. Bring the money to the bus stop on Old Bridge-Matawan Road, across the street from the church. Pull up in your car, get out and leave the money on the bench. There will be a gift waiting for you on the bench in exchange for the money. Take the gift, get back into your car and drive home immediately. You are being watched. Remember, no police. Complete this job successfully without incident and we will move on to the next one. Good luck."

At the time, I thought the best thing to do was to comply, so I did. I went to the bank, withdrew the money and followed his instructions carefully. It was a chilly, overcast day. Nobody was in town. The bus stop was set off the road a bit and was backed by woods. There were so many trees that the bus stop looked like it was going to be swallowed by them. I guess it was the perfect location for such an exchange. The package was there waiting for me as promised. I was thinking of just taking the "gift," jumping back into the car and speeding off without exchanging the money. I also thought of stuffing the moneybag with old torn-up newspapers, but I didn't do that either. I imagined he was there somewhere in the foliage watching me the whole time, peering down the scope of a hunting rifle. I mainly didn't want to do anything that would put Alyssa in jeopardy, so I went along. I got out of the car, put the cash down on the bench and picked up the package (a brown paper bag, rolled up tightly). I returned to my car with the package, got in and did exactly what I was instructed to do. I drove away.

Though I wanted to look in that bag right then and there, I was just as eager to leave that location. I felt his eyes upon me and it chilled my spine. The entire ride home I kept wondering what was in the bag. As soon as I pulled into my driveway, I tore open the bag and looked inside. At first, I thought it was empty. I reached my hand inside and felt around. I felt something, grabbed it and pulled it out. It was another piece to the puzzle. I looked at it for a while, but I couldn't make out what it was. This was another moment when I remained outside wondering, "Do I tell Kelly about this or is this something I should handle on my own?" After much thought, I decided this was something I should do on my own. I didn't want Kelly to be involved. She would only be putting herself at risk for no reason when I should handle it. I know her too well. If she found out about this, there would be no stopping her. She would do anything to save Alyssa, no matter how irrational or dangerous it may be. He said not to tell her about this so I decided to comply. I had to get our daughter home safely no matter what the cost, even if it meant lying to my own wife.

CHAPTER | 5

An entire day had gone. There was not another word from the police. I know they were keeping a close watch on the case, even if they did get my letter. It was just unsettling not seeing or feeling their presence. I didn't hear from the abductor either. I had a hunch that he was purposely remaining silent, trying to make me nervous and anxious. Periodically I would try calling the number he gave me, but it wouldn't connect.

I added the new piece I got from the bus stop to the puzzle, without telling Kelly. It fit right in the gap. It became clear to me, those missing pieces we were looking for, they weren't really missing. At that moment I realized, he has the missing pieces – and he's going to make me work for them.

The new piece didn't give any information that we didn't have before, but I knew what it was leading up to. By adding the missing pieces into this gap, we would reveal the man's face who is standing behind Alyssa in the picture, which I assume must be him. What didn't make sense to me is, why would he want to give away his identity? Once we know who he is, we can find him, get Alyssa back and he will be arrested. I didn't understand, but I went along. I wasn't about to psychoanalyze the works of a madman. I just wanted my daughter back.

Kelly and I didn't do much with Alyssa being gone. We didn't have a single thought without her. In such a state of mind, we both took a leave of absence from work, which basically means that I quit my job. Kelly is a star. She will have no problem finding a job if they don't take her back on the show, which I'm sure they will. For me, it's a different story. I'm just a cameraman. They'll replace me right away and, when I'm ready to come back, if there are no openings, I don't have a job.

We've had reporters and journalists calling and coming around, trying to get something for their stories but, considering the nature of the kidnapping, we didn't give any information and requested, for the safety of our daughter, that there be a media blackout. We didn't want any more reports on the case. We felt it would put Alyssa in harm's way. This was obviously a man who didn't want attention. Not at this stage in the game.

We avoided watching any TV, especially news. Most of the news is bad news, and we didn't need more of that. We tried to watch a few movies to get our minds off of everything for a while; otherwise, we would have driven ourselves mad. I never in my life had to choose so carefully what movies we were going to watch. We didn't want to see anything too serious that could echo our situation, but we didn't want to watch anything too lighthearted either because it might remind us of Alyssa. It doesn't matter how hard you try though. No matter what, you can't forget. You can't push something like this to the back of your mind.

We decided on *The Wizard of Oz*. That movie isn't too serious and it has no connection to Alyssa. She has never seen it before. It seemed like the perfect movie choice until we started to watch it. Then I remembered, "Oh yeah. This entire movie is about a young girl who gets taken away from her home to some strange land and is trying to find her way back to her family." I imagined, too, that wherever Alyssa is, it is just as confusing to her as Oz was to Dorothy, but not nearly as whimsical.

Just as they were about to meet the Tin Man, the doorbell rang. Kelly and I looked at each other confused. Neither one of us expected company. I got up from the couch, made my way over to the window and peeked out, not really knowing what to expect.

"It's the pizza man," I said with confusion.

That was probably the last person I would have expected at the door. I expected the police, reporters, even Alyssa's abductor before I would have expected the pizza man.

"You ordered pizza?" Kelly asked with a concerned voice, knowing I didn't really order pizza.

I walked over to the front door as Kelly watched from the couch. As I opened the door, the pizza man lifted the lid on the box.

"Sorry, bro. I was driving really fast to get here and the pizza kinda slid right off the seat. The cheese got a little messed up, see? All slid to one side and stuck to the lid."

There was, in fact, no pizza in the box. On the inside lid, three large letters were written in bold black ink on the cardboard box that only I could see: FBI. In the pizza box where the pizza would sit was a large envelope.

"It's okay," I said. "It's not that bad. I'll take it."

"You sure?"

"Yeah. It's fine."

"K. Thanks! It's on the house 'cause I ruined it."

"Thank you."

The man closed the box as I took it from him. I went inside, closing the door behind me.

"It was the FBI," I said as I brought the box over to the coffee table. I put the box down on the coffee table and opened it with Kelly. We went through the envelope and found a large stack of papers and a cell phone, exactly like mine. They instructed me to throw away my old phone and use the one they gave me. I didn't completely understand why, something about a tracking device and recorded calls.

Also in the envelope was a multitude of pictures to go through that were possible suspects. Some were people Kelly knew. Some were people she did reports on. Some were people I knew, and some people we've never seen before. It was very comforting to see that they were keeping busy with our case, even though they weren't visible most of the time.

Kelly began reading aloud to me a section of one of the letters written by Agent VanSlyck, the agent in charge, "Listen to this, 'He may have been aware of our presence at the bus stop because he never showed up for the money. We waited but when no one came, we terminated the operation.' What does this mean?" she asked.

"I'm sorry."

"What's going on?"

"I should've told you sooner. When I went to the post office, I came out and there was a letter on my windshield. It was a phone number."

I couldn't tell what she thought as I explained. The way she looked at me, was it fear? Confusion? Disappointment?

"The message said to follow the instructions and not to tell a soul. If I did, there would be consequences. I had to withdraw ten thousand dollars from my savings and leave it on an old bus stop bench. I guess they knew about it and followed me."

"He got the ransom, so now what? You gave him the money. Where's Alyssa?"

"In exchange for the money was another piece to the puzzle, waiting for me on the bench."

"Why is he doing this? I just want our daughter back!" Kelly exclaimed as a tear flowed down her cheek.

"I don't know, babe. I wish I did."

I pulled Kelly closer to me and hugged her.

"I want her back too. We'll get her back."

We fell asleep that night with tears in our eyes, but behind my tears was something else: Hope. With the FBI involved, I knew they would do everything they could to bring Alyssa home safely. We found comfort in that. In one of the letters, they warned us to be careful with what we say or do around the house because the kidnapper may have our home bugged with recording devices such as cameras or microphones. This could explain why he knows so much about us. They believe that he's been watching us for a long time before he took Alyssa.

They instructed us to be home the next day for a group of undercover agents who would be posing as carpet cleaners. They wanted to get into our home and search for any bugs that may be hidden. They were taking this case very seriously and were creative with ways to keep our communication open, even though the man who took Alyssa said that we must have not co-operated with the police. I felt like we were outsmarting him.

The next day, the FBI arrived posing as carpet cleaners all equipped and in cleaning uniforms. They came out of their *Glamour Shine* truck with vacuums, shampooers, sweepers, powders and air fresheners. I didn't think they were actually going to clean the carpets, but they did. They wanted to make it believable just in case her abductor was watching us as he said he was.

While they cleaned, they carefully searched the home for the possible recording devices that they mentioned in the letter. After a thorough search of the house, they found nothing. Once they knew the area was secure, one of the men handed me a case with my ten thousand dollars in it. They were there with me, watching and waiting for him to claim the money. They were going to follow him, but he must have known that they were there. He never claimed the money.

Agent Nikki VanSlyck sat down with us at my grandmother's lacey, cherry wood dining room table and went through the photographs with Kelly and me, discussing potential leads. We found a few men to be suspicious, but one particular man to whom we focused our attention. His name is Evan Abough.

Kelly's investigative journalism has won her many enemies for breaking news and discovering the secrets of people who hold positions of power.

Evan Abough is one of the many people that Kelly investigated, reported and ruined. He was a middle school history teacher and recently paroled sex offender in our community who was put away for seven years because of Kelly's investigations. He taught twelve to fourteen year old children world history, coached the softball team and was active in local community politics. The news came as a surprise to the people of the community because he was regarded as such a perfect citizen, always looking out for the children and his neighbors.

Kelly knew Mr. Abough personally, which is what began her investigation. They were not friends, just knew each other from the gym. His overly flirtatious personality and driving hormones steered him into inappropriate conversations with my wife nearly every time she went to the gym. She began to see what kind of person he really is. She felt that he was hiding something and putting on a front for the community and the school with his Mr. Perfect attitude. She began investigating and I guess the word spreads quickly amongst teenagers. Four girls, thirteen to sixteen years of age, stepped forward and openly admitted to engaging in sexual activity with Mr. Abough.

He was charged with all four counts; however, only convicted for two of them, the 15-year-old and the 16-year-old girls, both of which were statutory rape, admitting they consented have to sex with Mr. Abough. The other two claimed they were forced and manipulated by Mr. Abough, although there was nothing to substantiate those claims.

Evan Abough was our primary suspect for several reasons. The first being because he lives right in our community, he knows Kelly very well and has a personal vendetta against her. Those same suspicions apply to others such as Dr. Charles Q. Lundy, the doctor who Kelly busted for illegally selling prescription drugs to patients; however, the reason we focused on Mr. Abough is simply because he is a convicted sex offender. Though his students were not as young as Alyssa, it was still a terrifying thought.

The FBI decided to track Mr. Abough. They didn't want to make contact with him in fear that it would alert him to our suspicions and he would be more cautious with his actions. They planned to set up 24/7 watch on him, follow his every move, trace his every step and record his every breath. Without his knowledge of us watching him, they were sure they would turn something up and, if we're lucky, maybe he would even lead us to Alyssa.

CHAPTER | 6

KELLY

WHEN you have your face on television every week like I do, you're sure to gain a lot of enemies. I think that's just the way it goes in this business. For every couple of fans you have, you will have an enemy too. It's never something I put much thought into. I never imagined I would have someone hate me so much that they would want to do my family harm.

Being on TV was somewhat of a power trip for me. I enjoy exposing the private lives and dirty secrets that people keep. I am infuriated by the lies people tell to appear as an outstanding citizen of the community when, in fact, they are a vile human being behind closed doors. Calling them a human being might even be too nice. I am non-judgmental and maybe even more forgiving than most people, but that doesn't stop me from being sickened by their behavior.

I first started out working at a local news station in Iowa and I was never happy there. I always felt like I was too good for that place. Not too good for my town, I just had higher aspirations than local news. I wanted to make an impact on the world. I was reporting on fallen trees, floods, animal control problems, National Ice Cream Day, and other such "news" that made me feel like I was wasting my talent. Reporting on uninteresting events at a local news station is not what I wanted to do with my life. I didn't want to report the news. I wanted to break it. I didn't want to stand around talking about a fallen tree in somebody's yard from the latest tornado. I wanted to talk about the doctor illegally selling prescriptions to his patients, the school teacher sexually involved with his students, the strip club hiring underage dancers, the so-called coffee company importing bags of ground coffee that were really filled with cocaine, and other big stories like that which I could break. I wanted the news to be something that could lead to change or something better, not just reporting what happened once all the harm has been done.

Maybe that's why I have a lot of enemies. People see me as a pretty face on TV, only breaking the story for attention. I'd be lying if I were to say that I don't like the attention. Of course I do it for the fame and the money. That's why I went to school for performing arts. Ever since I was little, I always wanted to be on TV. I wanted to be an actress. I never considered working in the news industry. It wasn't until I got older and gained a desire to be constructive with my time in this world that I realized that I could combine my talents and compassion. By exposing the types of stories that I do, I help a lot of people in many ways, whether it is seeking justice or preventing more people from becoming victims.

I have always felt good about what I do. I never thought the day would come when one of these people would try to strike back. I suppose I felt somewhat invincible. Now I can't help but blame myself for everything that has happened. Not only is this in direct relation to my work because of Evan trying to ruin my life for ruining his, but also because I was never there enough for my family. I was consumed with my work and now my work has consumed me. I feel like it has swallowed me whole.

I suppose Evan feels betrayed for what I've done. He considered me a friend and it was as a result of my show that he got charged for those sex crimes against his students. No one would have known if it wasn't for me. The way he sees it, I stabbed him in the back. I never saw him as a friend. I saw him as a perverted, lustful, disgusting man. He and I were complete opposites. I think the only reason he was trying to be my friend was so he could sleep with me, even though he knew very well that I am married. In some way, that probably attracted him more. He seemed to like the challenge of trying to gain my interest. He wasn't going to let up until I gave in.

There wasn't one particular event that brought me to the decision that I should investigate him. It was over a period of time as I got to know him that I knew there was something not right with him. He would always choose the elliptical machine right next to mine, even if the rest of them were unoccupied. When women go to the gym, some of them wear extremely tight clothing and/or very little clothing. He made it a point to stare. He didn't just glance. He would stare so long that you'd think he turned to stone. His eyes burned through their yoga pants. I noticed that many of these girls he would stare at were at least half his age. I guessed he was somewhere in his mid-forties.

One day his sexism put me over the edge to the point where I couldn't help but say something to him. We were both on the elliptical, me on mine and he on his right next to me. In front of us was a girl, sixteen-years-old, wearing tight spandex pants. I know for a fact that she was sixteen because she was my neighbor's daughter and they just had a sweet sixteen party for her about a month prior to this incident at the gym. Her and her mother would come to the gym together.

For the entire forty-five minutes that he was on the elliptical, I did not see him once take his eyes off of her full, tight pants as she ran on the treadmill in front of him. I finished my hour set, thinking about how disgusted I was with him the whole time. I left my machine to get the disinfectant spray to wipe down the machine. When I came back, I looked at him and followed his eyes to the girl. I then looked back to him and said,

"You know she's only sixteen?"

He pulled his earbuds out of his ear and replied, "Huh?"

"She's sixteen."

"What are you talking about?"

"The girl you've been staring at for the last forty five minutes, she's sixteen."

"So?"

"You don't find anything wrong with that?"

"You're a woman. You wouldn't understand."

"Understand what?"

"She's ready to go, naturally, ya know?"

"No. I don't."

"Society makes up these rules of eighteen, not nature."

"So the rules don't apply to you?"

"I'm not saying that. I'm just saying, hundreds of years ago girls would marry by twelve. By eighteen, you'd be having your midlife crisis."

"This is what you teach in your history class?"

"Yup," he said with a laugh.

I didn't think it was funny. My response to him was a cold hard stare, just short of choking down my vomit.

"Lighten up," he said in a defensive tone. "I'm just kidding."

I left without saying another word to him. I suppose that if there was any one defining moment where I decided to investigate him, it was that moment.

I began by following him around, looking for suspicious behavior or some definite proof. I followed him for two weeks and never saw anything remotely interesting or beyond his normal routine to work, the gym and home. That was it. He didn't even go out on the weekends. I tried all different hours. I would sometimes follow him during the day or watch his house at night. I wanted to follow him around-the-clock, but I couldn't. I had my passion for my work, but the responsibilities I had for my home life were ever conflicting. I didn't watch him as much as I could. Things could have been slipping through the cracks. I knew I would eventually be in the right place at the right time. I felt it. I knew he was going to do something. I can usually tell when I'm following a dead end or heading for something big. This was significant. I knew it.

I got my first big break at the dawn of the third week. It wasn't hard evidence, but it was what I needed to keep me going. It was a lead. Directly after school, not long after Evan got home, a young woman walked up to his front door. She came from down the street with a backpack strapped to her back. I figured she must have come right from the bus and, rather than journeying home, she ventured to the teacher's house. She knocked and a split second later, he opened the door. I imagine he was waiting for her by the window so she wouldn't be standing outside for long.

She entered his house and vanished from my sight. The door closed behind her and the shades were tightly hugging the windows before she even arrived. I did not see what they were up to but I sat and I waited. She was in there for several hours. I figured she must have been lying to her parents about where she has been because she arrived at his house at two in the afternoon and did not leave until after six o'clock.

Even though I saw this girl enter his house and leave hours later, it was still not solid evidence that anything inappropriate was taking place. An easy line of defense would be that he was offering this girl tutoring, but there is no reason this needed to be done off of the school grounds and in the privacy of his home. Regardless, it was not strong enough for a report but enough to keep me searching.

I decided to follow the girl home but did not make myself known. Once I knew where she lived, I began making more leads; things started to come together. I still needed hard evidence and that was becoming increasingly difficult to obtain, but I never gave up. I knew that no matter how careful he was, he was going to slip up eventually. Everyone always does. Anyone who keeps at anything long enough is sure to miss a step. I just had to be there to catch it – and I was.

It was dark out with a low overcast sky. The blanket of clouds looked so close to the ground that if you just stretched your arms up and jumped, you could touch the bottom of the clouds with your fingertips. I sat in the front of his house in my car, parked across the street. I was waiting for her to leave the house, but she didn't. She was in there well after dark this time. Just as I was assuming they must have gone to sleep, I noticed a bright floodlight from the back of the house switch on and reflect off of the low clouds just above the house. I quickly grabbed my camera and got out of the car, curious to see what was happening.

I crossed the street and made my way along the fence to the very back of the property. Behind the fence, all the way in the back and directly behind the house was a gravel hill that led up into the woods. I climbed the hill and hid in the tree line, giving me enough leverage to see over the fence and enough coverage so I couldn't be seen. I positioned the camera against my eye and began capturing close-up shots with my telephoto lens. I got there just in time to see her strip off the last of her clothing and jump into the pool with him. Things became exceedingly more graphic as I tried not to let my rage get in the way of my journalism. Seeing that man performing such explicit acts with a girl more than half his age looked unnatural and sickening to me. My spine shivered.

Already knowing where she lives, the next morning I went straight to her house to speak with her parents. I had no idea what to say to break such difficult news to them, but I knew I had to go to them, considering that she was a minor and this was turning into a long term affair. Her mother recognized me from television as soon as she opened the door. She knew my show very well. I think seeing my face at her door already prepared her for bad news. She just didn't know how bad the news was going to be. I began by telling her the nature of the case that I was working on and that pretty much spelled it out for her. I did not need to get into any specific details.

It was a pretty quick decision for the girl's parents to press charges against their daughter's teacher, Mr. Abough. I got the exclusive story and interviews and that opened the floodgates on his case. More girls came forward right away and his story became one of my best episodes to date. It grabbed a lot of attention and drew a lot of controversy into the school system.

I know he must have felt embarrassed, angry, betrayed and especially vengeful for what I did to him. I never in my life saw someone so angry and so full of rage to take their vengeance to the level that he did. I never expected this is where my family would end up when I was thinking about our future on our wedding day. When we planned to have a child, I never expected someone to take her away. It's something we hear about almost daily in the news, but you never think that it's going to be your child. You never think that it's going to be your family that is torn apart.

It took a while for us to decide we wanted kids. When we first met, neither one of us wanted children. It seemed like so much responsibility when our lives were already so full. We didn't foresee having room in our lives for another obligation. It wasn't until after we were married that we first considered having kids. He was the one to bring it up in the first place. I really don't know what made him change his mind. For me, after hearing him talk about it, it got me thinking. I didn't want to get to the age where it would be too late and then realize that we should have had children. We really gave it a lot of thought before making a decision.

We didn't understand how hard it was going to be. After several unsuccessful attempts, we almost gave up. I didn't understand. People who don't want to have kids seem to get pregnant by accident while taking every precaution. We were really trying and nothing was happening. I thought something was wrong with me. What upset me the most was that we devoted so much time discussing it and changing our minds. We didn't want children at first and then convinced each other that it would be the best thing that ever happened to us. We went from not wanting kids to not wanting to be without them. After all of those long hard discussions, we were finally ready. We were more than ready. We were excited. We couldn't wait to start a family. It became such a frustration to me because of that. If we had just left the thought alone, we never would have known that we couldn't have children. Since we changed our minds, we saw that there was something wrong. We took it as a sign that we weren't ready or we weren't supposed to have children so we gave up and never mentioned it again.

We went on with our day-to-day lives. We both continued with our work, enjoyed our time on the weekends and had pretty good days. That's when we weren't too busy or thinking that there would ever be more to our family than what we already had. My mother kept asking us about when she was going to have grandchildren. We would just laugh it off. It seemed as though she would ask more and more after we stopped trying but, oddly enough, we never mentioned to her that we were trying or that we ever stopped. All she knew, as I have said many times in my life, was that I had no interest in having kids. I didn't want to live those nine months of agony to pop out many years of responsibility after that.

Life seems awfully unbalanced because it just throws never-ending surprises your way. When you think you get a leg up, everything you thought you knew turns out not to be so. It was four weeks after we had given up all hope that I found out I was pregnant. I didn't know. All that time, I was carrying our child and I had no idea. A whole month had passed before I realized. We had come to terms with the fact that we were never going to have kids. Once I learned that I was pregnant, I was really nervous about how he was going to take it. He even said to me, "I'm so glad nothing happened. I think it would've been a huge mistake. I guess it really wasn't meant to be."

I didn't know if he was serious. Was he saying that to me to make me feel better, to convince himself of that, or did he really believe what he said?

I thought of all the different ways that I could break the news to him, and then I realized that I was just thinking way too much. I was pacing back and forth in the living room, waiting by the front door for him to come home. I kept looking out the window for his car and, of course, this would happen on the day that he was running late. My anxiety was through the roof. I was a ticking time bomb waiting to explode the moment he got home. I was so nervous at first, not knowing how he would take it but the more I waited, the less nervous I became. My nerves started to transform into excitement once I realized what a blessing and a miracle it was, rather than focusing on what an unexpected turn of events it was. By the time I saw his car pull into the driveway, I was thrilled.

I told him the second he walked into the door. I don't think I even let him get the door closed behind him. I just blurted it out. He was slightly confused at first but had a hint of excitement in his voice. I'm not sure if he really believed me at first, but I'm sure he could hear the excitement in my voice. Once he believed I wasn't teasing him and it really was happening, he laughed as his eyes lit up like stars. His reaction was nothing I should have been nervous about. He grabbed me in a huge hug and squeezed me tighter than he ever did before. We almost lost our balance. We were both smiling so much it hurt as we shed a few joyous tears. It's the only time I've ever seen water fall from his eyes. I knew then that he was only trying to convince himself that we would be better off without a child. He really wanted it all along. It became very obvious to me at that moment that it was something he wanted more than anything.

"I guess it really was meant to be," he said.

CHAPTER | 7

JAMES

I am by no means close to anything that would resemble perfection. In the grand scheme of the universe, I know I am infinitesimally small in comparison. We come and go in this world, like the blink of an eye. In the billions of years this planet has existed, and the eternity in which was and always will be this universe, we are here only seventy or eighty years on average. In relation to Earth's life span, our individual lives last only a split second. A lot of things can change in a second. Sometimes it can change for the better, sometimes for the worse. In comparison to the age of our planet, our lives are like a split second, but all you need is a second to change the world.

I know I can focus on the negative side of things. I think we all do at some point. It becomes very easy for us. When I'm down about one thing, I can complain and come across as someone who finds fault in everything. It often becomes so easy to complain about the things that put a strain on me, but sometimes it's so hard to mention the things that pick me up. I just assume that people know how I feel about them. I think to myself that I don't need to tell Kelly that I love her all the time. I don't need to tell her that her smile, her soul, her whole self, has lit up every dark moment in my life. I assume she already knows, but, with that assumption, I have built up walls to divide us. She thinks the absence of words expressing my feelings is the equivalent to an absence of feelings. Sometimes it seems like we're running on a treadmill in our relationship. We just keep running and running but somehow we remain in the same place.

There was a time when we were moving at maximum velocity, gaining distance on our run toward the finish line. The words, "I do," are not the line in which we finish, but, more so, they are the line in which we start from. We didn't realize that. When the words, "I do," shot like a pistol into the air, we stood around like a couple of confused dogs at the gate, not noticing there was a lure to be chased.

It was a lot of fun when we first met. We were always making each other smile. We enjoyed finding new things that we had in common, even if they were simple things like realizing that Dobermans were both our favorite dogs. That's how we ended up with Daredevil. Ironically, we both always wanted a Doberman and never had one. We were able to get him as a couple. He was ours. There are a lot of things that we shared together. Everything was so exciting and new. Those things didn't change. I don't know why we changed. We still have all of those things in common. For some reason, just the smiles went away. Well, I know my smiles didn't go away. Maybe the smiles on my face did but not in my heart.

I'd hate to lose Kelly. All I have to do is look at her and I feel like I'm in Heaven. I can trace every inch of her body with my eyes and, even still, after all of these years, my heart beats stronger as my breath flows deeper. Simple things about her attract me: the way she pulls her golden hair up, revealing the back of her neck, the way her neck meets her shoulders, the way her body curves perfectly down to her hips, her strong legs, the way her ankles meet her heels, my eyes can just move in awe along every inch of her for hours. What makes me so attracted to her is not just the beauty witnessed by my eyes, but what she possesses deeper than what my eyes could ever see. She captivates me. Sparks fly within me just by the sight of her. I never tell her any of this though. I don't really know how. Like I said, I just assume it is known. Maybe not.

I look at her and partially what makes everything so surreal is that she was ever interested in me at all. I never saw myself as anything more than the average Joe. I don't dress flashy. I don't shave my chest. I don't wear any jewelry. I never realized until I met Kelly that you don't have to be a pretty boy to get a pretty woman. Somewhere, somehow, whatever it was that I had that was keeping her around this average Joe, I lost. Maybe it was the actions and not the words that she needed. She was in love with me not for the things I said. She loved me for the things I did. I'd like to think that she still loves me, but with the lack of words I am really not sure.

Through all of this, at least we have each other. In the heart of darkness, there is a light. That light is Kelly. I think she understood what that meant when I said to her, "You brighten my night." The night was analogously representing my somber mood and her soul, spirit, love, beauty, inspiration and all that she is which makes me happy is the light that comforts me. I think she got all of that out of one sentence. I hope she did.

Having Alyssa gone deepens regret within me because I didn't share many sentences like that with her either. My actions spoke love, but I never did. It's so hard for me sometimes to speak the way I feel aloud, but now with her gone and knowing I may never get a chance, it pains me more than I can say. It's easy to take things for granted when they are right under your nose. Our lives are often filled with trying to reach set goals, always trying to grab on to the next best thing, but we so often forget to be thankful and enjoy the things that we have right in front of us. I can't help but ask myself, was I there for her as much as I could have been? I guess we could always torture ourselves like that by saying that we could have done better. How often do we look back on certain events in our lives and say to ourselves, "Yup. I handled that perfectly. Wouldn't change a thing."? Rarely, if ever. It's because we grow and mature by the day, hopefully. I just pray that I get a chance to see Alyssa again and tell her all the things that I never said. I hope that I am able to. I hope that if any good comes from such a tragic event, it is that we grow closer than we ever were before. As a family, we need to take that second and make substantive changes to our world.

When we were failing at every attempt to have a child and when Kelly and I finally decided to give up, I wanted to cry every night. I tried to pretend that it was for the best. I lied to myself in order feel better. Somehow I thought that putting down the idea of us having kids would actually make me feel better. It didn't work though. I may have appeared to be okay on the outside, but I was depressed. I am an only child. Being unable to have kids would have meant the family tree would no longer grow. I wouldn't carry on our family name. I would never know the joy of being a father. I would never go to a dance recital or a football game. I would never record home videos of a birthday party or take a family vacation. I was going to be missing out on a lot.

Once I did find out that I was going to be a father, then the emotions really lost control. I was so excited. If I only ever witnessed one miracle in my life, this was it. I was happy. I was scared. I was excited. I was nervous. I wondered if I was really cut out to be a father. I was scared that my kid might not like me. I was hoping that I would be a good enough role model. Once I found out that it was happening, that's when I realized what a huge responsibility was growing inside of Kelly and once that responsibility came out, it would grow even bigger. As scared as I was, I think I was equally as excited. I just wanted to make sure I was able to give my child the best life that I possibly could.

Kelly got really weird when she was pregnant. Not in the typical sense of eating pickles and ice cream. She picked up a lot of new and interesting habits that lasted only while she was pregnant. She started collecting strange things and picked up unusual hobbies, like Origami – the Japanese art of paper folding. There's nothing wrong with Origami. I actually find it pretty impressive. One time when we were out to dinner she took a dollar bill of mine I was going to use as a tip and folded it up to look like a shirt. She also had an obsession with pet mice while she was pregnant and we had cages full of mice. Once Alyssa came, Kelly was back to her usual self. No more Origami, no more mice. I guess as a man, I will never know the physical and emotional changes that go on inside of a woman during pregnancy. I just had to support her and stick by her side in those interesting times. I still have the dollar bill Origami shirt in my wallet, but the mice have all died off.

I did my best to prepare for the baby, emotionally and physically. We got the room ready and decorated. I built the crib myself by hand. It gave me something constructive to take my nervous emotions out on. We packed a closet full of diapers and a cupboard full of baby food. We wanted to make sure that everything was ready. I don't think we missed a beat. We really worked well together while we were waiting for Alyssa to come.

I'm the one who chose the name Alyssa. Kelly and I had a long struggle with that one. She wanted to name her Ariel, but I really hated that name. It reminded me of the mermaid, the font and helicopters – aerial. She was really in love with that name and didn't want to budge on it, but I wasn't giving in. I just didn't like it. Eventually, she gave in to Alyssa because it was close enough. Now her name is Alyssa Ariel. We used both names. We just used mine first. Ariel is her middle name. It was a way to compromise.

As Kelly was nearing the end of her nine months, I became increasingly worried that I wasn't going to be around when her water broke. I wanted to rush her to the hospital with a suitcase just like they do on TV, but I knew I'd end up being stuck at work. I missed anything remotely interesting in my life because of my job and I knew that of all the times that the baby could be born, it would happen when they decide to send me out in the field and I'm a hundred miles away in the middle of a shoot. Despite all of my nervousness and worries, everything went over as smoothly as possible. Standing next to Kelly at her bedside was not easy. I guess being in the bed was worse, but it was so emotionally draining. As soon as that disgusting, fluid covered bundle of joy came out, I felt like I was ready to collapse to the floor in exhaustion. I thought every bone in my hand was broken. I was probably sweating more than she was. I was so glad that was finally over with. That was probably the emotional climax of my life.

Anything anyone ever says about baby stuff not being as bad when it's your child, they're lying. The white puke, the warm and squishy diapers, the horrible stench, the sticky toys, and the drool – it was a lot for me to handle. Sure, I love her to pieces but I just wished that she wasn't so messy. You would think I hit the lottery when Alyssa first used the bathroom by herself. I was very proud of her and really happy I wasn't going to have to touch another diaper. She had a flushing problem, but I'd much rather flush than wipe.

Aside from all of the responsibilities and disgusting things that come along with being a parent, I was really enjoying all of the rewarding things too. Kids can be a lot of fun if you have the energy. Having a kid brought the kid out in me. She was more fun than I had ever imagined. The gross things are still gross whether it's your kid or not, but the fun things – they are so much more fun when it's your kid. We did a lot. We really had a good time.

Another thing I was afraid of was Kelly and I losing our alone time together once we had a child. That did happen to some extent but not entirely. Kelly's mother, Paige, was thrilled to finally have a grandchild. Kelly was her only hope. Kelly, like me, is an only child. Paige was willing to baby-sit any time that we needed her to and would actually ask to take Alyssa off our hands. She loved having Alyssa around, and what kid doesn't like going to grandma's house to be spoiled with sweets and new toys?

For a period of time in my life, I was truly happy. Everything was pretty much just how I wanted it to be. When you have a moment in your life that is blessed with pure happiness, the hard times become so difficult because it becomes so easy to latch on to the past. Alyssa began having her health problems and that put a huge strain on us. Before our relationship had time to recover from that, things with work got more hectic. Kelly and I just fell further apart and things were never again like that fleeting moment of joy I once had in my life. I continually felt like I was fighting my way through the weeds, searching for my Eden.

I understand that being happy isn't living in a perfect world. If we wait for that, we'll never be happy. Things will never be perfect. It's possible to be happy while not having everything, but I'm just not there. I'm just not happy. I don't feel like I am the sole victim of unhappiness. I believe that most people think this way. We chase happiness like it is some ultimate, tangible goal but because we are always striving for perfection in our lives, it always seems out of reach. I'm not sure if we have control over our destiny. I used to think we did, but I'm not so sure anymore. I've heard the saying, count your blessings. In a sense, I guess that's true. You have to be grateful for what you have, but sometimes it's much easier to focus on what's lacking. I know that now, with Alyssa gone, any attempt to be happy will be futile. In retrospect, I had very little reason to be unhappy. I'm reminded of another saying: you never really know what you have until it's gone.

CHAPTER | 8

IF I am angry with the human race, then our creator must be livid. It is time for reevaluation and a major change. What kind of world do we live in where one human being steals that of another? A man takes what is not rightfully his, a child, a soul of her own in the natural care of her parents. He not only stole our daughter but stole from her too, her innocence and her childhood. What manner of world do we keep in which such monstrosities not only exist, but happen daily at a steady pace? What are these evil people doing in a world amongst those of innocence who are subjected to a world full of horrors and punished by such demonic behavior?

I used to believe that life is a learning experience. We are put here by God to grow, spiritually. We are presented with challenges in which we must overcome in order to break through the other side stronger than we were before. The problem is, what if the challenge presented is bigger than we are? How do I overcome something that I can't seem to get a grasp on? Is faith alone enough? I do believe faith alone can take me a long way, but I also believe that God has empowered us all to stand up and fight for ourselves with him by our side. I don't think I'm supposed to sit around and do nothing, waiting for Him to take care of my problems for me. Will-power and the human desire are very strong forces, giving us mind over matter and the ability to do what is otherwise impossible. We cannot leave everything up to God. He gave us independence and free will because he expects us to use it. He wants us to use our brains, our hearts and our souls and not rely on him for everything.

My heart is filled with desire and the will to get Alyssa back, no matter what the cost, even at the expense of my own life. I am not afraid to die. Determination replaced sorrow. Faith replaced anger. Heroism replaced cowardice. Strength replaced weakness and courage replaced fear. Determination, faith, heroism, strength, courage, in my body, mind and soul, in every cell pumping through my veins, ready to bring my daughter home.

I was ready for the next piece of the puzzle. This time I felt more powerful and confident than ever, knowing the FBI would be there with me, hiding in the shadows. I felt invincible. When he called me, his accent spoke to me once again over the phone through a pre-recorded message, providing instructions for what I must do next. I felt secure knowing that the FBI was hearing every word being said. His message was carefully articulated like he sat for hours crafting it, perhaps on a piece of paper filled with scribbles and corrections in search of the best words to say. It sounded like he was reading from a piece of paper.

"Your job is to tell everything I'm about to say to you to your wife, Kelly, because in the words I'm about to speak to you, you will hear instructions for her and her alone. She must complete the job alone without your help, without the help of anyone. That includes the police, the sheriff, the FBI, the carpet cleaners and the pizza delivery boy. Your daughter is alone. She is not being cared for. Paige is alone, too, in another location and also unattended. No meals. No water. Your time is limited. One of two things will happen. You will follow my instructions carefully and complete the puzzle, revealing where to find them or you will not follow my instructions, the game will be over and they will die alone because you don't know where to find them. It is up to you whether they live or die, not me. Remember these instructions perfectly. That is your duty. Then it is your wife's to carry them out. She is going to need a brown box. In this box she will put Kristy, Alyssa's Teddy Bear. She will also put in that box your daughter's purple blanket, a few pairs of comfortable pajamas, socks, slippers, sneakers and her blue coat. Along with this box, you will also bring back the ten thousand dollars. These items are to be taken to the same location you dropped the money off the first time. You have three hours."

That was it. That was the whole message. It was becoming clear to me, beginning in that very moment, I could no longer play by the rules. He was playing a game. He didn't have any real demands. He has Alyssa locked away in some dark basement all alone. He doesn't care about her blanket and teddy bear. These were all things to keep us distracted. What he really wants is to see us fail. Playing his game by his rules, that's what we will do – fail. It was time to play by my rules. I was not going to let my daughter sit alone and die while we put together a jigsaw puzzle.

The best way to beat someone at his own game is to think outside the box and catch him unawares. Like any good sport, the way to win is to watch for mistakes and take your opponent by surprise – a surprise left, a blitz or a fake handoff, a twirl or a behind the back pass, whatever it takes to win. It was time to throw him a curveball.

I had it all planned out. I filled the box with rolled up newspapers and sealed it shut tightly. Along with that, I brought the same bag the money was in, but filled that with newspapers too. He wanted Kelly to deliver the boxes? Fine. No problem, but I was there first, hiding. I knew he had to show up eventually and I wanted to be the one to catch him. I told nothing of my plan to Kelly or the agents involved. I knew that they would only try to talk me out of it. I had my mind made up. Nothing they could have said would have made me change my mind.

Kelly put the boxes in her car, unknowing that they were filled with newspapers, and headed for the bus stop, but I was already gone. I told her I would be with the FBI. Instead, I hid in the woods behind the bus stop on Old Bridge-Matawan Road, where the original handoff was. I looked around but I didn't see anyone. I didn't see any signs of him, or any signs of the police. The deserted bus stop and empty street was reminiscent of a ghost town in a classic Wild West movie. An old newspaper on the sidewalk picked up by the wind blew across the street like a suburban tumbleweed.

It was at that moment, my cell phone rang. I answered.

"Hello?"

"What are you doing?" asked the man's voice.

"Who is this?"

"I clearly said your wife, Kelly. Not you. Why are you here?"

"I'm not."

"Don't lie to me."

I looked around everywhere but I didn't see another soul in sight. It was just the floating newspaper and me. I was hiding deep beneath two thick bushes in the woods behind the bus stop. He couldn't possibly see me.

"Listen to me!" I shouted into the phone. "I want my daughter back! I'm not playing your games. She is my daughter and whatever it takes, I'm going to win this!"

"You will get your daughter back. It's very simple," he said with a frustrated tone. "You do as I say and she will return home safely. Don't do as I say and she will return home to you – piece by piece! I guess it depends on how you want her back."

I hesitated for a moment as I looked carefully at the bus stop. Just as the time before, the brown paper bag sat waiting on the bench. I hung up the phone, sprinted out of the bushes and ran for the bag. Suddenly, as I ran toward the bus stop, I heard the popping sound of shots firing at me. I ducked, not knowing where they were coming from, but I did not stop running. I grabbed the bag as the shots continued to fire and the bullets ricocheted off the metal bus stop enclosure.

I ran out from under the enclosure and started running fast down the street, just as I saw Kelly pulling up. I flagged her down as she approached. She slowed the car down but I jumped in before it came to a stop.

I slammed the door and screamed out to her in a panic, "Go! Fast!"

"What's going on!" she shouted as she heard the shots.

"Drive! Now!"

Kelly stepped on the gas with a hard kick as the tires slipped and screeched beneath us. She firmly held control of the wheel as the car sped away. Kelly looked into the rearview mirror as shots were bouncing off the trunk of the car. She punched the gas and went faster as we approached a red traffic light.

"Don't stop!" I said. "Turn left here."

Kelly made a sharp left and turned down the side street to avoid the red light.

"What's going on?" she asked.

"He knew I was there."

"What were you doing there?"

The phone rang, saving me from answering her question. I picked up the phone.

"Where do you plan on going?" asked the man on the phone.

"Why would I tell you?"

"You can't hide from me."

"You're not gonna win this!" I emphasized again.

"That's where you're wrong! Stop now or I send the first piece of your daughter home to you in a box!"

I became silent.

"What's he saying?" Kelly asked.

I continued to sit in silence, unsure of what the next move would be, but I knew it was my turn. I thought for a moment, rolled the dice and continued the game.

"You're bluffing," I said as I hung up the phone.

Kelly frantically questioned me, demanding to know what was going on.

I took a long deep breath. "He's trying to regain control. We're in control now."

"What's he bluffing about?" she asked.

The phone rang again. As it rang, we sat in silence as I ignored it.

I turned to her and said, "Nothing. He'll do nothing."

The phone chirped its final ring and became silent. The only sounds to be heard were the steady, faint passing of the wind and the thumping and buzzing of the tires on the road. I wish I knew what to do. I wish I had all the answers and the heroism of Bruce Willis to win this fight, but I had to come to a realization. I'm not an action hero. I'm just a father and a husband who wants the very best for his family.

From behind, the flashing lights of an unmarked police car rapidly approached. Kelly hesitantly slowed down and looked at me, as if she was gauging to see if she was doing the right thing. With no opposition from me, she pulled the car over to the shoulder and brought it to a stop.

Two agents jumped out, ran up to our car and pulled us out.

"Come with us!" shouted one of the agents. They kept our heads down and covered us as we ran to their car. They helped us into the back seat then quickly closed the doors, got in and sped off.

"The bag!" I yelled in a panic.

"I got it," the agent said as he began unrolling the top of it. The other agent glanced from the road to the bag and back again. He kept doing this with his curious eyes, trying to get a peek inside of the bag while keeping his eyes on the road.

"Who are you?" Kelly asked.

The man driving responded, "I'm Agent Zimmerman and he's Agent Spencer. FBI, working on your case."

Agent Spencer added, "We're the ones, well, the few of many, who have been following you around to keep you safe."

"And I nearly got shot," I said.

"But you didn't. So, you're welcome," Agent Spencer responded.

"What were you doing?" asked Agent Zimmerman. "You put yourself and your daughter in a lot of unnecessary risk."

"Did you get him? He was right there. He was at the bus stop," I answered.

Agent Spencer pulled a puzzle piece out of the bag.

"That's it?" asked Agent Zimmerman.

"That's it," Agent Spencer responded.

Kelly leaned forward to look at the piece and said, "That's the second one."

Two pieces, neither of which provided any insight into the bigger picture, which made me realize, I did the right thing. He was just wasting our time.

They took us back to the police station and brought us in to view the interrogation room from the opposite side of the glass. Sitting on the other side was the man who abducted Alyssa. Orpheus Dunedin, fat, bald and sweaty, yet cold like a block of ice, is the man who opened fire on me at the bus stop. Although he attempted to flee after firing the shots at me, the police caught him rather quickly after a short chase on foot.

It wasn't easy to come by his name. He carried no ID, but what he did have was a set of fingerprints and a criminal record. Mostly a thief, Orpheus robbed a couple of banks, a jewelry store, got busted for carjacking and even did some time for attacking a woman with a knife.

In addition to the fingerprints, they found a boot print. The boots were inspected closely in comparison to the muddy prints that were lifted from the carpeting in our home, left the night my daughter and mother-in-law went missing. After careful investigation, the print and the boot were deemed a perfect match. Orpheus is the man who took Alyssa. This meant no more puzzles. No more clues. We won the game. There he sat, in custody. All we needed from him was to know that she was safe and where to find her. I was optimistic, too optimistic.

The game wasn't over. Not for him. He didn't speak a word and this is how he continued to play. He had seemingly gained the upper hand. I thought he would try to deal for information, but he didn't. He remained silent.

I wanted to jump right through the glass, smash that man's fat head into the table and demand he tell us where our daughter is. All the information, right there, an arm's length away and we didn't know any of it. He kept it in his head. The interrogators were doing all they could but nothing would make him talk. He didn't speak a single word, not even to ask for a lawyer. He remained as silent as a stone. Behind those eyes, locked away under his tongue, were the secrets that remained unspoken. I watched infuriated as the man sat expressionless and motionless. Not a word, not a murmur, not a gesture, not even a blink was exhibited. He sat, looking away at the floor, as if his body was there with us, but his mind was elsewhere with Alyssa.

The police asked us if we recognized him, if we knew who he was or if we thought there would be any reason why this man, Fat Orpheus, would take our child and Kelly's mother, and kill the dog. Neither one of us have ever seen nor heard of Orpheus Dunedin. He was a stranger to us. I could only imagine what he wanted with Alyssa. The scariest thing about it to me was that this man was a total stranger, never once have we laid eyes on him; however, he knew everything about us. He must have been watching us for a very long time, planning to take Alyssa and just waiting for the right moment without us ever knowing. I can't help but wonder if there were signs or clues that I missed, anything that I should have picked up on to protect my daughter. I searched my mind for any strange events in the recent past or if I may have seen this man in passing anywhere before. Nothing came to mind. He was like a ghost, a shadow, an enigma – but as long as he is captivity, I am sure he will not remain a mystery for long.

CHAPTER | 9

It was kind of strange sleeping next to Kelly again, because we never actually made up or talked about the problems we were facing in our marriage. The problems we faced as parents were much more important and made everything else so trivial that any other problems we had seemingly didn't exist anymore. We had a common interest, to get our daughter back safely. It hit Kelly really hard and she needed me. I wanted to be there for her, and I was. She cried a lot that night. The reality of the situation was beginning to set in as the shock wore off, especially after seeing the man who took our daughter face to face. Kelly tried hard to keep it together, both for her daughter and her mother, but even for the strongest among us, it's easy to be overwhelmed by emotions.

I didn't like seeing her like that and I certainly didn't like feeling so powerless. I wish there was something that I could have done. I did all that I knew how to do and it really wasn't that much. I wanted to be the hero – the one who beat the bad guy at his own game and saved the day – bringing our daughter home safely, carrying her in one arm as my face is covered in dirt, with the building where she was kept burning down to the ground behind us as I walk away, carrying Alyssa.

Once Kelly had fallen asleep, I slowly and quietly made my way out of bed. I crept my way through the bedroom and over to the master bath where I locked myself within. The nightlight dimly lit the room as I sat myself down on the edge of the tub. I put my head in my hands as the tears were raining from my eyes. Cries of thunderous sorrow surfaced, wailing from within. I never cried once in all of my adult years, not even when my grandmother died, but as I sat there and thought of Alyssa and Kelly and all they were going through, I wept enough to build oceans with my tears. I knew there was nothing I could do. I don't know if Kelly heard me crying that night and I pray that she didn't. As the man in the family, it is my duty to keep strong and hold it all together, but I just couldn't hold it in any longer.

I couldn't help but keep thinking, why me? Why Alyssa? Why us? Why is there such evil in this world and how do we overcome it? Questions raced through my mind faster than I could get the answers. In fact, none of them were answered.

Orpheus Dunedin. I feel like I've seen the devil. What's wrong with this world when humanity works to destroy itself? From the big things to the little things, people have no regard for one another. No decency. No respect. We are not all kidnappers, but we all have a lot of room to grow. How many of us can not only admit that to ourselves, but also recognize where those changes need to be made, then make them? Not many.

I don't understand the things people do. You see in the movies all the terrible, disgusting, graphic horrors and chaos but to be quite truthful, none of that compares to what a real person is capable of in all actuality. I wish I understood how people like murderers, rapists, child molesters and kidnappers – how can they do all the things that they do? I saw on the news an old man who was shot. How can someone shoot an 80-year-old man in the back of the head, never knowing his name – a man who has never harmed a fly, a man too weak to fight back, a man too weak to run, a man who just falls flat on his face from the bullet shot from behind, a man women and children and grandchildren will weep over in mourning? There is so much horrific news. How can someone cook a live cat in the microwave just to see what would happen? How could someone put a 4-year-old child in a dryer and turn it on, letting him die, just for his own sick amusement? Working in the news industry, I see this as part of my daily routine.

This is real. Real life. Out of all the movies I have seen, none are as evil or unjust as real life can be. These stories don't have Hollywood contrived happy endings. They end sadly. They end tragically. Why do people take pleasure in that which is evil? Why do people have cold hearts and closed minds?

Even down to what is seemingly the simplest thing, there's evidence everywhere that some people care only about themselves. When I took a visit to the restroom at the police station, I was steadily pondering the decency of humanity, having just met my daughter's kidnapper face to face. As I pondered this in the restroom, I noticed a chewed up piece of gum in the urinal. This is a sign that whoever was chewing this gum is a man who cares about absolutely nothing or no one other than himself. Why? Because a chewed up wad of gum is not going to flush down a urinal, especially when there is a plastic guard there, preventing solid objects from flushing down the drain. Now some poor sap is required to reach his bare hand into the urinal and pull out a used, chewed up wad of gum saturated with urine that people have been peeing all over the entire day. All he had to do was turn 180 degrees and take three steps forward. There's the garbage can. Now spit. This angers me because this person is so self-absorbed that he didn't think about, or didn't care about the man who has to go fishing with his bare hands for a urine soaked wad of chewing gum.

That's far removed from child abduction, I know, but my point is, big or small, we all need to take an extra second to think about what we do and how it affects everything and everyone around us. It's time to think about more than just ourselves. We live in a culture that is too self-absorbed. There are people out there who can't walk, can't use their arms and can't even speak, confined to a self-powered wheelchair for their entire lives, but they are just so happy to be alive; yet, your average person will have a bad day just from getting up on the wrong side of the bed without even considering that it is a good day, just for the fact that they were able to get themselves up out of that bed. We are all guilty of it. We are all victims of this self-absorbed society.

I, for example, tend to let things go around the house. I would be over-whelmed with my responsibilities and then I would get lazy. I would tell Kelly that I'd fix the leak in the tub. I'd promise to sweep the floor while she would clean the kitchen. For one reason or another, it would never get done. I was the King of Excuses. That's one thing. I need to do what I say and stop being a procrastinator.

Sure, that's not as bad as cooking a cat in a microwave, but my point is, I can do better. I can make Kelly's life easier, and that's just my point. Shouldn't we all strive to be better? Shouldn't we all try to make each other's lives a little easier and more enjoyable? In the grand scheme of things, wouldn't we all be a little happier then? I know if I were the best that I could be to Kelly and she were the best she could be to me, our separation would not have happened.

I know this all seems very trivial but my point is, as a whole, humanity has a long way to go and, though you may not be able to directly improve a kidnapper or a murderer, you can directly improve yourself. If everyone became a better person, somewhere down the line, maybe we'd all become a little more pleasant. In a more peaceful world where people cared for one another, perhaps there wouldn't be so much violence. I know that would never work, but sometimes I enjoy retreating to a utopia in my mind where a peaceful, non-violent world exists where all of us get along in love and harmony.

I live in a world inside my head where the weather is beautiful, not a cloud in the sky. I launch down the slide in our back yard with my daughter in my lap as we laugh. Kelly brings out a pitcher of iced tea with a lemon slice garnish, wearing her hot pink bikini top with a tropical pareu around her waist, a little pink flower tucked away behind her ear, accenting her flowing blonde hair, gently blowing in the warm breeze. Daredevil is there, entertaining himself with a Frisbee as Kelly's mother, Paige, is there to help Alyssa off the slide once we reach the bottom. Life is beautiful inside my head.

This man, Orpheus, came and took that beautiful life away and now I can't find it anywhere I look. I see his face in my mind, Alyssa alone in some musky dungeon with no light, a child who is already afraid of the dark. I don't understand what this man wanted from us, or worse, from Alyssa.

The sun blazed through the window in our upstairs bedroom, but the searing golden light illuminating the world around us was not nearly enough to break us from our sleep. With all the stress and worries wearing us down and keeping us up, we finally crashed into our dreams. I had nothing but nightmares about Alyssa and her kidnapper. They taunted me and made me want to avoid my sleep. I would analyze these dreams for answers or clues but they were just dreams and I never found any of it helpful. I guess I was hoping it to be like those psychics on TV who help solve crimes. That's either not real, or my dreams don't work that way. I guess I'm not psychic, just troubled.

Not long after I had fallen asleep, both Kelly and I were awakened by a hard knock on the door and the bell. I got out of bed and squeezed moisture drops into my dry, tired eyes then made my way down the stairs. I opened the front door and there stood a parcel deliveryman with a box and an electronic pad for me to sign.

"Who sent this!? Where did it come from!?"

The deliveryman looked back at me like I was a raving lunatic and asked, "Is there something wrong?"

"Yeah. I need you to tell me where this box came from!"

"Right here," he said, pointing to the return address. "Bob Smith. Eighteen sixty five Lincoln Boulevard, Toms River, New Jersey."

"Where's Lincoln Boulevard? Who's Bob Smith?"

"I don't know."

"What's your name?"

"Tom McCullough."

After getting his name, I signed for the package and he went on his way. He seemed a little confused about my attitude, but I'm sure he sees all kinds of strange people in his line of work. I wasn't sure if I should open it first, find out who Bob Smith is or call the police, but I already had a pretty good idea of what was in the box. By this time, Kelly had been standing across the room, looking at me in wonder as I stood silently with the box.

"What is it?" questioned her curious lips as the words fell upon my deaf ears. I looked away from her and down to the box. I carried it to the kitchen table, threw it down and rummaged through the drawer for the scissors. I took out the scissors and carefully cut the box open. I lifted the brown paper inside to find within a handwritten letter and a clear plastic sandwich bag. Kelly, still standing across the room, couldn't bring herself to step closer.

"What's in the box?" she asked.

With a pause and a collapse of breath I began to read the letter aloud, "You were warned. Follow my instructions and your daughter will return home safely. If not..." I stopped reading.

"If not, what?" she asked. I remained silent as Kelly asked again, "What does it say?"

"If not, I promised to you that she will return home," I swallowed my tears and took a breath, "piece by piece."

Kelly panicked and began to cry as I too had tears streaming down my face. I continued with the letter, "Just so we are clear, this is the first piece."

I took the sandwich bag out of the box. The bag contained a lock of hair.

"You have to do what he wants," muttered Kelly through her cries.

"What he wants? I don't even know how he sent this. I'm doing what I can. I'm trying to bring our daughter home!"

"I want my daughter home in one piece, not in boxes!" Kelly screamed out as she fell to her knees, grasping the back of the chair and sobbing with tears.

I walked over to help her up, grabbed onto her arm and she cried out, "Get off of me!"

"I'm trying to help you!"

"Just leave me alone!" She screamed.

As I pulled back my tears and cleared my mind, I realized three things. I first realized that she needed some time by herself to cry and let it all sink in.

Secondly, I became aware, just then, that even though we are faced with new and more traumatic problems, that doesn't mean the old problems of our marriage or separation had just gone away. I guess I thought that magically our complications wouldn't matter anymore once we were fighting for a common cause, to bring our daughter home safely. Suddenly, we'd be on the same team, fighting together, rather than against one another; but, just like in our marriage, Kelly and I have very different ideas about which is the best way to handle things.

The third thing I thought was, where did the hair come from?

I was shaking on the inside, holding my composure so Kelly did not see me weep. She needed to know that I was strong, strong enough for the both of us; but, when I arrived upstairs, I closed the bedroom door behind me, turned the lock and rushed my way over to the bed where I laid down flat with my face in the pillow, bursting into muffled howling cries of anguish.

I swam in my tears, throwing my fist with anger into the bed. The wailing of sorrow turned into cries of infuriation and back again. I was fatigued with emotions, flooding my heart, my mind, my body and my soul.

As the tears ceased, I rolled flat onto my back and watched the ceiling. I looked through it. My eyes were open but my mind was somewhere else. I wasn't thinking about a thing, nor was I conscious to the world around me. It was as if my body was a breathing slab of meat lying on the bed.

I was conflicted. I was losing my grip. I was breaking down. How long can a man pretend to be strong when his only child, his little girl, has been taken away? I can't imagine, I don't want to imagine, what she's going through. Hasn't this poor child been through enough? In just four short years, almost five as her birthday approaches, she has already battled cancer and is now put through this. Rather than spending her fifth birthday with her family and friends, unwrapping dolls and plastic kitchen items, eating cake and running around like a sugar addict, she will be confined alone in a dark room. I can't get that image out of my head. A little girl, so filled with energy and life, confined to a chair in a dark basement. If he sent that puzzle to trouble us, then as hard as it is for me to admit, he was successful. What evil can be so heartless to harm a purely innocent child?

I walked over to the closet and removed her birthday gift from the top shelf. She had been bugging me about flying a kite ever since she saw a father and son flying one in the park. I bought her a red, blue and yellow macaw. It's supposed to look like it is in flight. She loves animals, especially birds, so I thought it was the perfect gift. Looking at it was such a strong symbol to me that she is gone. As I sat in the chair across the bed with the kite in my hands, I thought about the possibility of never flying it with her and if – WHEN (I'd like to think) she survives this, my poor little girl has a lot to overcome. She, in her adult life, will have a lot to deal with. There's no way of knowing now the many different ways this may affect her later in life. I know that it will, but how she responds to it will most likely not be positive. Can anything positive be taken from a situation like this?

Alyssa is unquestionably bright for a child of her age, the shining star of Intellectualand, nicknamed Inteland, Alyssa's pre-school. She's smart. She's quick witted. She knows the difference between right and wrong and stands up for what she wants, but that's not always a good thing. I just hope she stays out of trouble.

I think one of the things I miss the most about her is when I would look down at her and she would have her arms reaching up to me, looking at me with those big green eyes, saying, "Up, please." When she would say it, it sounded more like one word, "Uppeeze!" She would always over emphasize the word please because we taught her that it is a polite word to use when you want something. I guess she overemphasizes it the more she wants something. I would lift her up and she would wrap her arms behind my neck and lay her head on my shoulder. I miss holding her hand. I miss her begging for candy before dinner and me telling her no. She always did what she was told. I miss making her breakfast. She was picky and hardly ate anything I gave her, but I still loved making it for her. I miss the happiness she brought to me when she would first see me and, filled with excitement, her mellifluous voice would call out, "Daddy!" as she ran to greet me with a warm hug. I miss laying on the carpet in front of the TV, watching cartoons with her as she used me for a pillow. I miss having to wash my hands every five minutes from picking up all of her sticky toys. I can't imagine never seeing her again.

When Alyssa was born, I had an image in my head of how she would grow up to be. I know parents who visualize their children as adults are rarely correct in their projections, but you can't really help but wonder and hope for the best. I pictured the day I would dance with her at her wedding. Now I won't even help her blow out the candles on her fifth birthday.

In life, we are forced to make a lot of choices. We could just let go and try to let the choices make themselves, but from the experiences I've had in my life, I am witness to the fact that if we don't want chaos to linger over our heads and through our lives forever, we must make our own decisions. Sometimes they are simple. Should I have coffee or juice with breakfast? Sometimes they are difficult. Do I really want to get married and have children or do I want to remain single and focus on my career?

Do the decisions that we make today mold the rest of our lives? I used to think that we could ruin our lives based on one bad decision, but lately I have been questioning if that's true. Is there such a thing as a good decision or a bad decision or does life find a way of balancing itself out, regardless of the decisions we make? What if the day I met Kelly at the fireworks had turned out differently? I chose to pursue Kelly even though my friend was trying to fix me up with her other friend, Mae.   It's impossible to know how one decision can affect us over another because once the decision is made, you can never go back in time to that moment to make the choice again.   I never question my decision to be with Kelly. Although we've had our rough times, there is no doubt that I always knew that she is the one.

I used to spend so much time looking at door number one and door number two, expecting one to be a blissful paradise and the other to be an enveloping black hole that descends deeper into the darkness for eternity; however, what if door number one and door number two are actually the same? Although what is beyond the two doors may look strikingly different, if you strip away all materialistic observations, perhaps the raw emotion is exactly the same for each. Maybe life has certain lessons we are meant to learn in order to help us develop and no matter what decisions we make, circumstances will be the same, even though we perceive it as a choice.

I cannot think of any decisions in my life that I have made which turned out to be truly good or truly bad decisions. Was marrying Kelly a good or bad choice? I've had the best times of my life with her and never felt such love for anyone before and we have a beautiful daughter who means the world to me. On the other hand, Kelly and I are slipping away and my daughter is missing. If I never got the chance to know Kelly, would I be saying the same things about someone else? Maybe good choices and bad choices don't exist. Maybe there are just choices. I just hope the universe is smart enough to balance out all of our stupidity.

I don't know what choices I have to make now. I hear the world all around me: the birds, they sing all of their colorful songs, variant in their voices to perform a heavenly choir; the people go on about their lives, each to make decisions in what adventure will be brought to them today – all I wonder is what adventures Alyssa will be facing today and will all the right choices be made to keep her safe.

CHAPTER | 10

EARLY in the morning before the sun rose, I was awakened by my thoughts. A drive to the local store and a tall caramel cappuccino was a sad attempt to ease my nerves, waiting for the hour in which the church doors would be open. I took my coffee and my thoughts to church early.

I sat with my car across the far end of the parking lot, backed to the woods. I watched over the church grounds, witnessing the cold wind blowing gently through the grass. I watched as it lightly shook the dead branches on the trees. I slowly sipped my steaming caramel cappuccino while I squinted my eyes upward through the windshield, looking at the clouds floating slowly in the sky.

God spoke to me through these things of his creation. The gentle breeze lightly blowing symbolized to me the hardships we were going through, but its gentleness in nature told me that it would all be okay. I find comfort in church sometimes. It can help me see things a little more clearly. I'm not one who visits a church on a weekly basis, but I go when I need it. I believe that God is everywhere and that I don't need to go to church to talk to God; however, I do believe that the fellowship of likeminded individuals can be really powerful and uplifting. Being away from it too long also puts God in the back of my mind. I often get to the point where I don't know what to believe anymore, if there even is a God. I hold on to hope, but sometimes it's really not that easy.

The thing is, I wasn't going to church that day for the service and it wasn't Sunday. I was waiting for the priest, Father Emerson, to arrive from the rectory to open the church doors. I sat and I waited.

Every move made thus far by Alyssa's abductor has been an attempt to obfuscate our dilemma with a charade of riddles and mysteries. We were all sure that Orpheus was not acting alone. Receiving contact from this mysterious stranger via the letter and the lock of hair was his way of showing us that Alyssa remains in danger and his capture was inconsequential.

What we did know is that whoever sent us the package, the mysterious stranger, was not the one, "Bob Smith," written on the return address label, addressed for return to 1865 Lincoln Boulevard in Toms River, New Jersey. It was a fictitious address, just as the name in which our mysterious stranger bares. More games. More lies to throw us further from the truth. 1865 Lincoln Boulevard, from my searches, exists only as a strip mall in Santa Monica, California. To my surprise, the irony that it exists at all, considering 1865 was the year Abraham Lincoln was assassinated, was very unexpected.

As I remained in my deep thoughts with my eyes eclipsed, the church doors opened with a gasp. Father Emerson, standing in the doorway looking out to the lot, exhaled a hurricane of apprehension so strong that I felt it from where I sat. I could tell this was something he was afraid to do. Before retreating from the doorway, Father Emerson slapped on an ostensible smile, masking the unsettling shake he felt within.

He turned back through the doors and disappeared into the dark shadows of the church. As I watched him vanish into the darkness, I sipped one final sip from my tepid caramel cappuccino, realizing that my racing heart was not from the caffeine pumping rapidly through my veins. It was the same anxiety I knew Father Emerson concealed with his illusive expression to the sun, before retiring into the womb of the church.

He waited for me inside the church, within its enchanting halls; a sanctuary for disheartened souls. I carried myself like my burdens, heavy footed with courage, from my car, across the lot and into the church. I piled my hopes and prayers atop the astronomical mountain of words in line for the Lord to hear.

Once sending my prayers away to the Heavens, I stood from the altar and turned around. Father Emerson greeted me with disconsolateness, sorry for what my family has been going through, and also lent me his prayers.

I reached into my pocket and pulled out a sandwich bag with the folded up letter and the lock of hair sealed within. I handed it over to Father Emerson. I thanked him, blessed him and thanked God for people like him in this world, the counterpart to those like Orpheus and our mysterious stranger.

When I asked him why he chose to help us, possibly putting himself in danger, he stated, "If I pray for the good of the world to overcome evil, I cannot stand idly by when the Lord provides me the opportunity to participate in the very thing I was praying for. My prayer to stop such evil has brought you to me."

With a letter of such and a lock of hair, the fact that we were still being watched closely was clear. In order to protect my daughter, I knew I had to play by the rules, which plainly said I must have no contact with the police. That's when

Father Emerson stepped in as our courier, the bridge between us and the police.

When I arrived home from church, I saw that my prayers had been answered. Sitting atop the slide in our backyard, all dressed up in her pale blue puffy winter coat and bundled in her pink hat, scarf and gloves, Alyssa slid down the slide out of sight, disappearing behind our honey oak stained fence. I leapt from my car and ran to the fence, pushed open the gate and ran into the back yard with a dash.

"Alyssa!" I shouted as I ran toward her. She was squirming herself from the bottom of the slide, barely mobile in her bundle of winter gear. I approached her, got on my knees and helped her off of the slide. I turned her around to give her the most joyous hug and kiss I had ever given.

"What are you doing?" Kelly asked.

I pulled back from the hug and looked at Alyssa. "Danielle?" I said, in confusion.

I looked to the back porch and saw Kelly and our friends, Melissa and John. Melissa is a short and pretty woman with dirty blonde hair and a sporty style, wearing a New York Yankees jersey and a pair of jeans. She's not a flashy woman. She doesn't wear fancy clothes or much makeup, but she is a natural beauty. John is a man physically as large as his heart, and he's got an enormous heart. His generous proportion is tall and heavyset but powerful. His style is tame, nothing flashy – bearded and wearing jeans and a flannel shirt tucked in.

"Why is she wearing Alyssa's things?" I asked.

John, intercepting my question, replied in his deep, Herculean voice, "I'm sorry. She wanted to play outside and I asked for them. It's my fault."

"It's fine," I said.

That was a very embarrassing and frustrating moment for me, to think I had my daughter back and, right in front of everyone, I made a fool of myself. With that, I got off my knees and walked into the house through the back door, walking by everyone in shame with my head down.

One could not tell from looking at me in that present moment, standing motionless in the kitchen and hidden behind a wall in embarrassment, that there was a tumultuous war raging inside of my head. I was so upset that Danielle was wearing Alyssa's clothing. I was ashamed for displaying my weakness on my sleeve. I was overcome by sorrow because it was not my daughter playing on the swings, maybe even a little jealous, too. The disturbance inside my body was a furious assault on my senses that bludgeoned my head like a pounding mace, thrashing my brain. I felt the pumping and swelling in my head with a vertigo effect as I grasped the counter, white-knuckled. The room moved out from under my feet and swayed back and forth like an old ship sailing through a wicked storm. Upon the shifting of the room, it disappeared before my eyes. Staring forward with my eyes wide open, all I saw before me was black. Darkness. I saw nothing. It felt like someone strangled a chord in my brain, causing me to collapse like a dead weight to the floor.

When I opened my eyes, it felt like only a second had passed. I was disoriented and dizzy. As I tried to sit up, John shouted out, "He's all right!"

I heard him shout, though it sounded faint and far away to me. I was still coming to. I was lying on the couch in the living room. He sat on the edge of the coffee table next to me. I could barely see the glass of water he was trying to hand to me because my sight was still a little blurry.

"Drink this," he said, attempting to wrap my hand around the glass.

"What happened?" I grabbed the glass of water, slowly sat up and sipped it.

"You passed out. I carried you to the couch. I saw you going down, but I didn't get around the counter in time to catch you."

"How long was I out for?"

"Not even five minutes. You should lay back down."

I took John's advice, handed him the glass of water and lied back, easing my head into the pillow.

"You're lucky you didn't hurt yourself. You fell hard."

"   Did Kelly see me?"

"Fall? No. She saw me carry you to the couch. She was really concerned."

"Where is she?"

"In the kitchen with Melissa fixing Danielle some tuna fish. She's making you a sandwich too. I figured you'd want to pull yourself together first before she saw you."

"You know me too well."

"How are you guys doing, I mean, with each other?"

"Well, been better. Been worse. It's been a long time since she and I shared any real connection. At least we're living under the same roof again; but, given the circumstances, we didn't really have a choice."

John looked at me, not knowing how to reply. I continued, "Every once in awhile, when things are really tough, we do need each other, and I don't know about her, but I can feel it, that spark, my love for her. We were holding each other one night, the first night she was here, and that was the first time I felt that spark again in a long time. It's like we put aside our differences for Alyssa, ya know? Like our own problems didn't matter anymore."

"So what then?"

"I don't know. It's just not the best time to bring it up. She has enough problems, and anyway, things aren't perfect. We hardly communicate and we still fight."

"But the spark is still there?"

"Yeah. For me."

"Well, don't let it turn into ash and dust again. Tell her how you feel. It may be exactly what she needs to hear right now. Suppose this is the right time, right now, and she's thinking the same thing about you, 'He's too stressed to deal with our petty problems. He's only going to start an argument.' Look at Melissa and I. You think we're always happy? Of course not. No couple is ever perfect. The thing is, we communicate. That's how we stayed together. Through it all, we love one another and from what you're telling me, so do you and Kelly."

"Yeah."

"So would you like to prove you could be a man? Open up to her. Show her you're not afraid of your emotions. That's a real man, not someone who closes up and pretends to be tough. You gotta lighten up."

I laid there thinking about what he said. He was right about everything. It takes a stronger man to open up and tell a woman how he really feels. A weaker man is one who tries to act tough and lock away what is really in his heart. That's not a sign of strength; it's a sign of weakness. Even though I knew what he said was right, I froze and locked up, just like I always do. I crawl into my emotional shell, thinking that's going to protect me from getting hurt or feeling any sort of negative emotion that I don't want to feel. All it really does is hurt those around me and make everything worse. I guess I never really understood that. I always regarded myself as being in touch with my emotions and communicative, but John made me realize something. There's a difference between a man-to-man talk and dialogue with your wife. When it comes to talking about how Kelly feels, how I make her feel, that's when I don't want to talk anymore.

"Well, regardless," John continued, "it's nice to see you two under the same roof again." He stood up and walked away.

Kelly and I have known John and Melissa for quite a few years. We always pictured ourselves to grow old as life-long friends, being those old folks who take Atlantic City bus trips together to see Tom Jones and gamble our Social Security money away on the slots and video poker. Melissa and Kelly would go play bingo at the local firehouse while John and I would sit on the front porch drinking Scotch and smoking cigars, yelling at the young kids too close to the lawn. That's how it was supposed to be. When Kelly and I split, that was a huge blow to our friendship. Although John doesn't admit it, I think a big part of what kept his marriage with Melissa together is the friendship and bond between the four of us. I think he was afraid that it was all falling apart, first our marriage, then our friendship, and then his marriage. I'm not sure if he wanted to see Kelly and me back together for us or for them. I guess for all of us. Either way, he is my best friend and always will be.

Kelly and I being separated could get a bit tricky around the holidays. Between the four of us, we really don't have much family left, if at all. We were each other's family. We spent all the holidays together, all of them, down to Halloween. Alyssa and Danielle would dress up in costumes and the four of us would take them around the neighborhood trick-or-treating.

This was the first time we've seen Melissa and John in awhile – the first time since Alyssa went missing, even the first time since the separation. That wasn't commonplace for us, considering we would get together on almost a weekly basis. Months had passed before they paid us this visit, understandably though. It would have been a difficult friendship having to teeter back and forth between Kelly and me, trying to balance an even and fair friendship with both of us. I guess with the separation fresh in everyone's mind, it was the time we needed to figure out how to handle the situation. Upon learning about Alyssa's disappearance and all of our family's misfortunes, that's when friends must come together for what truly matters.

Kelly entered the room carrying a plate of my favorite lunch, tuna on toast and a heaping pile of sour cream and onion potato chips. I smiled as I sat up and she smiled back. Her smile melted my heart. She set the plate down on the coffee table and I planted my feet on the floor, sitting in front of my plate.

"How do you feel, sweetie?" she asked.

"I feel okay."

"What happened?"

"I don't know. I just got light-headed."

"Well, finish your water and eat. Maybe you'll feel better."

I reached for my plate and began picking from the fries.

"Aren't you eating?" I asked Kelly.

"In the kitchen. I'm going to eat with them. I figured you'd want to rest a bit by yourself, unless you want me to join you."

I hesitated for a moment, not knowing what the correct answer to that would be. Should I ask her to join me? Does she really want to or is she just being nice? Does she really care or does she just pity me? All of these thoughts without a single answer between the questions, I blurted out to her, "No. It's okay. You go ahead and eat in the kitchen."

"You sure?"

"Yeah."

With that, she stood up, leaned over and gave me a kiss on the cheek with my mouth full of food.

"Enjoy your lunch, babe. Feel better," she said as she walked away.

I turned around as she walked away. I watched her leave the room and my heart sank in witness of her beauty. I wanted to yell out to her but couldn't. I wanted to tell her that I changed my mind. I really did want her to join me for lunch. I didn't want to appear so indecisive or needy, so I said nothing. I turned back around and took a bite of my sandwich. As I was chewing, I thought I could take my plate and join the rest of them in the kitchen, but I thought that would be weird having already started my sandwich. It was too nerve racking. It was too much pressure. I was thinking too much. Instead, I sat in the living room by myself and ate my tuna on toast alone.

CHAPTER | 11

NIKKI

I started working for the FBI when I was 29-years-old. That was thirteen years ago. It was my dream ever since I was in high school to work for the FBI. What first appealed to me was the way the bureau was depicted on television and in the movies. I looked up to the agents with great respect. They were smart. They were tough. They were cool. They were heroes. Being in the FBI would be my chance to be a real life hero and help people. When I was born, the FBI was strictly a male organization. Not one female agent roamed the halls or the streets. Today I am one of the hundreds of female agents in the FBI.

I work with the Crimes Against Children (CAC) Program. This includes sexual abuse, violent crimes and kidnappings. I work as part of the Child Abduction Rapid Deployment (CARD) Team. Under the "Lindbergh Law" Congress gave the FBI jurisdiction to investigate any reported mysterious disappearance or kidnapping of a child of or about the age of twelve or younger. There doesn't have to be a ransom demand, the child does not have to be missing for twenty-four hours and the child does not have to cross state lines. This was not always the case.

On the evening of March 1, 1932 in East Amwell, New Jersey, Charles Lindbergh, Jr., son of the world famous aviator Colonel Charles Lindbergh, was taken from his home. This was handled by local law enforcement between New Jersey (where the child was taken from) and New York (where the child was being held). What fascinated me most about this case is the way the kidnapper communicated with the family by placing letters under rocks and delivered by a taxicab, with all communications back being printed in the newspaper.

Like many other kidnapping cases, the letters indicated a ransom demand. What had me perplexed about my case is that Alyssa's abductor seemed to have no specific demands. It's not unusual for a child to be abducted for reasons other than a ransom. There are times, unfortunately, when children are abducted and their kidnappers have no intentions to return the child. The difference with those cases is that the kidnapper never contacts the family and usually stays out of sight.

We have a monumental amount of evidence which all points to Orpheus, the man in custody. A security camera outside of the post office clearly shows him placing the initial letter on the car's windshield. The voice on the phone is an obvious match to anyone's ear, yet further analysis needs to be done for evidence. He was placed at the bus stop during the money drop. His boots match those muddy prints that were lifted from the scene where Alyssa was taken. The evidence pointing to Orpheus as Alyssa's abductor is overwhelming, but there's one piece to the puzzle that doesn't fit – the hair that was sent back home in a box from "Bob Smith." It's a perfect match.

How do you explain having the obvious abductor in custody and then receiving a package bearing a false name, which includes a lock of Alyssa's hair? First, I thought the obvious answer was that he wasn't working alone. It seemed as though this was a scare tactic, a forced improvisation to frighten the family into complying and proving that Orpheus is nothing but an unimportant pawn in his game. In other words, Orpheus has just been doing the legwork for whoever hired him, the one who goes by "Bob Smith."

Another theory I had was that perhaps Orpheus sent the package himself before we had him in custody. The final theory I had was that he contacted someone on the outside and asked his contact to send the hair as a diversion. By doing this, he thought he would throw us off track.

I started my search by looking for Mr. Evan Abough, the schoolteacher, who was our original person of interest. My suspicion for Mr. Abough increased when he was nowhere to be found and no one has seen him for days. Though an interesting discovery, it abolished our plans to survey his movements and behaviors. We set up a twenty-four hour watch on his house. No one came in or out and not a single light ever came on.

In the meantime, agents canvassed neighborhoods, followed leads and hit one dead end after the next. I decided to visit Mr. Abough's place of business, now a small factory where he is part of a team that manufactures commercial grade air fresheners for hospitals and the like. Since being charged and convicted in his child molestation case that Kelly cracked open, he is no longer eligible for employment as a schoolteacher working with children.

I spoke with his supervisor at the manufacturing plant to find that Mr. Abough has been on a week-long vacation and has not been into work. We asked around at the plant, but no one knew of his vacation plans. They knew he was taking time off, but he never said where he was going. According to most people there, he is a quiet man who keeps to himself. He comes in, does his work, takes his breaks and goes home. He doesn't work too hard. He doesn't slack off. He's there to do what he's supposed to do and that's it – nothing more, nothing less. After exhausting all of our options, the only thing left to do was to be convincing enough to gain a search warrant and turn his house upside-down and find any leads to his whereabouts.

Once we were inside his home, we did a very thorough search. We looked in every room in every corner, every drawer and every box. We gained access to his computer files, but there was nothing to link him to this case; although, we did hit a gold mine to charge him with something different. We obtained a heaping pile of evidence to prosecute him for child pornography. There was nothing to indicate that there was any connection between him and this abduction, but bringing him in on the pornography could bring us one step closer.

Being a mother myself, it's really hard sometimes, but I think that's also part of where my passion for this work comes from. It makes me absolutely sick to see pictures like that. I didn't even want to know what was on the videotapes. I couldn't imagine someone taking my children away from me. That's why I work so hard for the families. It's unsettling to think that people ever have to worry about things like this, but it happens so often.

I'm not always successful and that really upsets me. I want a success story every time. Who wouldn't? Unfortunately, there are some cases that just go cold. Others turn up a body. I don't know what's worse, giving up or finding the child is gone for good. Until you have a body, families hang on to the idea that their child is still alive, even if all evidence points to the child being deceased. I can't blame them. I would too. I often wonder, if I was the parent, what would I rather? Would I rather the case go cold and never know what happened to my child, or would I rather find out my child has been murdered? Is ignorance truly bliss? Ignorance is the brain's incapacity to have the best interest of self in mind. Ignorance is disastrous. Enlightenment is bliss; the power of knowing better than a dog chasing its tail. It's with enlightenment comes responsibility. That's why I think some people just feel better off not knowing. Sometimes I think there are things that we believe we need to know. Once we know the answer, we don't want to accept it. The human mind is a peculiar organism.

The worst part of my job is telling the family that their child is dead or that the case is going cold. The best part of my work is when I get to tell the family that we found their child. That's why I do this. I just wish we found every child we looked for. I sometimes imagine it's just not meant to be, but I will never understand why an innocent child has to become a victim of such a merciless crime. All I can do is keep fighting it and hope I win. I hope I win this one.

CHAPTER | 12

JAMES

SOMEWHERE in recent history, though I'm not quite sure of the defining moment, the depravity of human nature has propagated like a virus. Maybe it has been since the beginning of man, slowly through the generations, we have lost our morals and good wholesome values. It often seems like animals act more civil these days. A snowball has rolled into an avalanche.

I don't know why I was there, but as I stood outside Mr. Abough's home, all of these things haunted my mind. I didn't think I was going to find my daughter there. The police already searched his house. It wasn't that I thought the police weren't doing their job. I thought they were doing a good job. I was just looking to understand. I thought that by being there, maybe I could feel what it is like to be such a man. If I understood that, I might understand several things, including where he might have my daughter and how I can begin to forgive him. I thought I might find some meaning to why a man would involve himself in such salacious acts with children. I have seen the branches and the leaves, but I wanted to see the root of evil.

The night was late and dark with a cool foggy mist in the air, only seen beneath the dim yellow street lamp. I stood outside his green ranch house. The lawn was a landscaper's nightmare, overgrown with weeds and uncut grass. I was dressed all in black so not to be seen.

I glanced around. Nobody was watching. I heard wet tires in the distance, splashing their way closer up the street. I ducked behind a tall evergreen tree as the car passed by at a steady pace. Once the car was out of sight, I hopped the fence and disappeared to the back of the house. The backyard was big and secluded from the neighbor's view. There was no grass or plants. No flowers. No trees. No bushes. There was nothing but rocky gravel leading up to the fence, surrounded by woods. Off the deck was a pool, enclosed in a chain link fence and surrounded by a cement walkway.

Once on the deck, I approached the back door. The sign on the door warned, "Restricted," indicating it was a crime scene. The door was bolted shut so I jerked open the kitchen window and climbed in, stepping into the sink.

I stood in the kitchen for a moment as the eerie wind blew outside the open window, blowing the curtains in the breeze through the moonlight. I pretended I was this man, Evan Abough, a seemingly normal and upstanding citizen of the community within those walls. I closed the window and stepped out of the kitchen. The dining room was part of the kitchen and opened to the living room to my left. I didn't turn on any lights because I didn't want to make my presence known to the neighbors or a passerby. I navigated my way through the dark home, using the rays of blue moonlight to guide my way. Nothing seemed out of the ordinary, just any normal man's home. Tasteful furnishings. Nothing classy but not a dust bomb either. I used the light on my cell phone to pan the room, looking to see any items that may be hidden in the shadows, away from the moonbeams. There was nothing particularly out of the ordinary; however, I believe that if there were anything of the sort, the police would have already taken it for evidence.

I walked down the hallway and peeked my head into the bedrooms. One looked like an office, the other for storage and the master bedroom was obviously where he slept. I stepped into the master bedroom and looked at his bed. I wondered if that is where he defiled the young girls. I tried to imagine what it was like for him. What enjoyment did he get out of it? Why? Why did these underage girls consensually have sex with their teacher? Was it always consensual? I could speculate, maybe it wasn't even the sex that got him so excited. Maybe both Mr. Abough and his students enjoyed it because it was something they weren't supposed to do. I honestly see nothing natural about a man in his forties having sex with a fifteen-year-old girl. They knew it was wrong and maybe that's why it felt so good to them. Instant gratification. I know he must not feel good about it now. That gratification was short lived. His whole life was turned on its head. He lost his job. He lost the respect of the community. He went to prison. He's not allowed anywhere near the school. Maybe the problem is, people live in the now, not thinking about the future. Maybe there's something missing in their lives and they try to fill that emptiness inside of them with something superficial. They fill themselves with darkness rather than light. I guess we all do that in some way. I went there trying to find answers, but still all I had were speculations.

I walked to the closet and rummaged through some boxes, searching for anything. I knew the police had already turned the place upside-down. I don't know what I was looking for. I just thought by looking, it would make me feel better. Look at me. I tried to fill myself up by searching in the darkness, rather than looking in the light. There I was trying to find the root of evil by breaking into someone's house. To find it, I shouldn't have been looking at everyone else, but within. That is the root of evil, within us – within all of us. Perhaps it's our very curiosity with good and evil which makes us eat it all up like a vanilla chocolate swirl – light and dark, good and evil, consistently entangling themselves within us.

As I was digging through the box, I found a photograph of a young child, no older than twelve, stripping from her bikini. What would a forty-something-year-old man be doing with a photo like that of a twelve-year-old? I took it with me into the bathroom where there was more light. I noticed he took the photo on his deck. Where would one even get pictures like those developed?

There was the sound of a car door closing as I stood there in the bathroom. I quickly threw the picture into my pocket to hide it and ran out of the bathroom into his office. I peeked through the blinds and saw Mr. Abough walking up the sidewalk. I realized I didn't have enough time to run back into the kitchen, climb out the window and make a run for it without being seen or heard.

He noticed the police posting on the front door then nervously looked around. I knew the police had bolted the front door shut as well, so I knew he wasn't getting in. Then he walked toward the window I was looking out. I jumped back and ran into the hallway. I thought he saw me. I prayed that he didn't. I stood with my back against the wall in the dark hallway, breathing deeply and muttering under my breath my hopes that he did not spot in his home. I peeked my head around the corner to watch his shadow move against the translucent window shades as he tried to open the window. I realized then that he didn't see me. He wanted to get into his home for another reason.

His shadow moved across the window and disappeared. I waited, but he did not return. I peeked out the window again and saw his car was still in the driveway. I knew what that meant. He was going around to the back of the house to find another way in.

I ran to the kitchen to lock the window, but it was already too late. The moment I stepped into the kitchen, I saw him walk by the window. He jiggled the lock on the back door and hit it with what sounded like a rock. The door rattled on its frame as the walls shook from the force as he slammed his body into the door and tried to kick it in. He was determined to get into his home.

As he was busy trying to break through the back door, I took that opportunity to quickly run into his office again. I knew if I wanted to get out of there without being seen, that was my only chance. A part of me wanted to wait until he came in so I could attack him by surprise. I wanted to know where Alyssa was, even if I had to beat it out of him, but I knew he wouldn't talk. I would just get myself in trouble for being there. That's why, in a split second, my mind formulated a plan.

I got on my knees in front of the window in his office, unlocked it and slid it open. I pushed up the screen, hopped out into the bushes and closed the window behind me. As long as he didn't notice the window being unlocked, he'd never know I was there, unless he looks for the picture that I still had in my pocket. Perhaps if he did, he'd think the police had it along with the rest of the evidence.

While he was looking around inside, I ran to my car, which was parked down the street by a patch of woods. I got in and, without turning on my lights, pulled up close enough to the house to see when he would leave; however, I made sure to stay far enough away so he wouldn't see me. I waited quite a long time. He was in there for longer that I suspected he would be. I guess he wasn't concerned with anyone catching him in his own home in the middle of the night.

Time drags at a snail's pace when you are just waiting for it to pass. At such a late hour, I was struggling to stay awake. I feared I would fall asleep and miss his departure. I turned the car back on and froze myself with the air conditioner in order to keep myself up. I would have turned the radio on too, but I didn't want to give away my presence because of blasting music.

Finally, as I could no longer keep my eyes open nor keep my head up any longer, bright reverse lights striking my eyelids alerted me. He backed out into the street and drove away. I rolled my car forward and, as he got far enough ahead of me, I turned on my lights. I've never actually followed someone without wanting to be seen, especially in the dark with my headlights shining. I didn't know what I was doing and I was nervous he was going to see me. Regardless, I kept my distance and tried my best not to lose him. I followed him to a location downtown, not far from the bus stop. That time of night, especially in the winter, it was a ghost town. We were by the bay where people would launch their boats in the summertime, but now they were all up and out of the water for the winter.

He got out of his car and walked up the sidewalk toward an old Victorian home, across the street from a deserted bait and tackle shop. The pink Victorian home had been converted into various offices. I noticed on the sign out front that it offered a dentist's office, hair and nails spa and a few other businesses that were written in smaller writing that I couldn't see as I drove by.

I parked my car around the corner and made my way back to the house on foot. As I approached the building, I carefully looked around while staying on the dark side of the street to make sure he was inside. I saw his car parked out front, but all the lights were out in the building. I tried to see if he was sitting in his car, but it was so dark that I was unable to tell. I decided to cross the street and walk by his car as if I were just taking a nightly insomniac's stroll. As I approached the car, I saw that it was empty. I made my way up the lawn and around to the back of the house.

When I walked around to the back, I noticed a light on in the basement. The small flimsy rectangular windows were at the ground level so I laid myself down on my stomach and crawled to the side of the window. When I peeked in, I saw Evan Abough ripping photos down from a clothesline and dumping photo trays filled with chemicals into the sink. He was in a photo lab cleaning up. No one just cleans up that late at night.

It seemed obvious that the police didn't know about his photo lab so when he saw that they searched his house, he rushed to hide the evidence at his lab. Afraid of the evidence being destroyed, I pulled out my cell phone to capture some images. I put my phone into camera mode and snapped the first photo. Unaware that the flash was on, the window lit up with a burst of light. I rolled away from the window quickly and covered my hand over the light, afraid that the flash alerted him to my presence. I looked at the picture and saw that it was nothing but a bright white reflection on my hand. I hastily turned the flash off and prepared to take another picture. I rolled in front of the window but hesitated when I didn't see him in the room anymore. I snapped another picture of the empty room and then quickly got up, ran to the side of the property and hid behind a bush. That's when I saw him come around the back of the house to the window and look around, expecting to find the source of the flash. He must have seen it. I would have snapped another photo, but it was too dark outside. My screen showed nothing but the blackness of the night.

I stayed hunched over behind the bush, waiting for him to go back inside. I wanted to get better pictures. He stood by the window while his eyes scanned the entire area. He panned his head as he glanced along the edge of the property. He locked his eyes on the bush that I was hiding behind. He was staring at the bush. I stood motionless like a statue and didn't breathe. I didn't even blink. He squinted his eyes in the darkness. I remained like a rock, unmoving. He turned around and headed back inside. I stayed in my position until he was out of sight. I slowly peeked my head around the bush. When I was sure that he was gone, I slowly made my way toward the window again, remaining in the shadows.

I got my phone ready to snap a few more photos but as soon as he got back into the room, I saw him walk straight in toward the window and pull the curtain over.

I missed the opportunity to catch him in the act, but I was able to obtain proof that his photo lab existed. I was excited that I was making progress in the case, that I wasn't hopeless and counting on everyone else to save my daughter. I felt like I was participating again. Active participation in my daughter's life has always been paramount to me, especially when she is in trouble. It took a lot of self-control to not attack him and threaten him. I wanted to make him take me to Alyssa, but I knew that he wouldn't. As tempting as it was to go after him, even if just for the sake of revenge, I knew the best way to find Alyssa was to stay in the shadows and let him lead us to her.

CHAPTER | 13

I went straight home that night, but I didn't tell Kelly where I was. It was never my intention to tell anyone but once I saw the dark secrets of Mr. Abough, I knew I had to tell Agent Nikki VanSlyck. I planned to visit her first thing in the morning to tell her about his basement photo lab.

It was hard. Pushing it to the back of my mind made me feel like I was keeping dark secrets of my own from Kelly. My shame would not let her know that I was snooping around like a rat between the walls. The truth is, I had something else on my mind. Losing my wife and my daughter at the same time was more than I could take, more than any man could take. Unlike my daughter, my wife was right there in the room. I realized that I was trying so hard trying to get Alyssa back, slipping in and out of the shadows, but Kelly was right there in front of me. Getting her back, our marriage back, I thought that might be something I could possibly accomplish with greater ease. It was something more tangible within my grasp.

Kelly and I were in our pajamas. She had just brushed her teeth and was coming out of the master bathroom, heading for bed. My mind was racing and my heart was pounding as I sat in the chair across the room, watching her slide under the covers.

I knew if I didn't say something that very moment, just like always, I would never say anything. So many times in my life I've been so close to saying things I wanted to say, things I should have said, and then never say anything. Spontaneously, I said, "I have something on my mind."

She did not respond. The whole reason I said that was to throw it out there in such a way that I would be forced to expound. Without a response from her, it became ever more difficult to say what was on my mind. She seemingly didn't care. I let out a deep, exhausted sigh, stood up from grandma's old floral patterned chair and headed for the door.

"Where ya going?" Kelly asked.

"Downstairs."

"You're not telling me what's on your mind?"

"I didn't think you cared."

"I'm waiting for you to tell me."

"Oh."

I slowly made my way over to the bed where she laid with her back rested against a pillow on the headboard. I sat myself on the bed by her side.

"Do you ever still think about us?" I asked as I looked down, away from her eyes. "I'm going crazy thinking about you. I keep having these thoughts that someday we'll put all our differences aside and just be like we used to. Whenever I think about my future, it's not just mine. It's ours. I can't picture life without you. I know we're separated right now, whatever that actually means, but I feel like you're mine and I'm yours."

I paused a breath and waited for her to respond, but she said nothing. I thought that she might have confused my serious question for a rhetorical one so I continued, "I just wonder," but she interrupted me and said, "Please don't do this to me now."

"So you don't feel the same way?"

"It doesn't matter. That's not what's important now."

"When will it be important? Why isn't it?"

After sharing nothing but the silent air, without an answer, I knew it was time for me to leave. I spent that night downstairs in my grandfather's old bedroom trying to figure out why this is unimportant to her. My grandmother and grandfather slept in different rooms. When I was a child, I thought that was normal. I thought when people grew old, they lived in separate rooms. It wasn't until my teenage years when I realized something was wrong. Perhaps they didn't get along. Maybe they didn't love each other anymore and, being strict Catholics, didn't believe in divorce. Maybe they did their best with the situation. For all I know, it could have been as simple as grandpa's snoring wouldn't permit grandma a decent night's sleep so they decided to sleep in different rooms. I never knew the reason and now I never will. What matters to me is that Kelly and I don't turn out the same way.

As we went to sleep in separate beds, I wished it wasn't so. I didn't want our marriage to end. I especially didn't want our love to end. This is far from how I pictured my life, sleeping in my grandfather's bedroom away from my wife, during our separation as we both struggle with the loss of our daughter, hoping and praying everything is okay. What happened to the house, the dog, sending Alyssa off to school with another child on the way? All of that changed.

This is a marriage deprived of any affection, a once enchanting romance that has receded into a timorous despondency. Sleeping in the room of a man who died alone in this bed while my wife lays wide awake with vacillating thoughts roaming about in her head was a sure way to drift further apart.

My bedroom door whispered open and Kelly stepped forward with a light knock.

"You asleep yet?" she very quietly asked.

"No."

"Can I come in?"

"Of course."

"How are you feeling?" she asked as she stepped in and softly shut the door.

"Okay. You?"

"I don't know why, but as much as we fight, as annoyed as I get, I still feel a burning in my heart for you."

I pulled the blanket up and made room for her on the bed. "Come here."

She made her way into the bed and under the covers with me as I wrapped my arms around her and pulled her head into my chest. "Kelly, I love you."

She smiled but gave no response. I didn't blame her. I continued, "Though we never seem to get along lately, argue about nothing and annoy each other to no end, my heart never stops loving you. I still think about us and miss everything that we were."

"I want to fix that, I think – the not getting along part," she said.

"Me too."

"How?"

"Well, you took the first step by coming down here, not going to bed angry or alone."

"That's not going to solve the problem."

"What exactly is the problem?" I asked.

"Miscommunication? Mistrust? What else?"

"Misunderstanding."

"How do we fix it?"

After I thought for a second, the answer seemed obvious, "We start communicating, we start trusting and we start understanding."

"How do we do that?"

"We start with the first one, communication. I think we're doing that right now."

She leaned closer and pecked my lips with hers. She stayed in bed with me all night. It was a faraway dream that someday all of our problems would be washed away, but that night, though far in the distance, the dream was visible on the horizon. A soft gentle kiss, long enough to show we care upon our goodnight, claims true to the fact that neither one of us wished to see our love fade. The briefness of the kiss, the clear fact that it did not last any longer, told us that we were only on step one. It didn't bother me though. In order to climb to the top, you have to take that first step.

I'm not sure if I ever really knew any couples living the dream at the top. Reaching the top may actually be an unobtainable goal, but it's imperative that we try. To just live within the parameters of the present state of affairs, what then would make us any different than a prosaic android? Our wants, emotions and desires are our make-up concerning a life worth living. Life is the active process of living, all the moments we experience in the adventure of pursuing our dreams. Without such, we do not live.

CHAPTER | 14

KELLY

THOUGH I closed my eyes that night, I did not go to sleep. I was asking myself, does he really feel this way? Maybe his feeling of need for me is a way to patch the gaping hole in his heart made by the loss of Alyssa. The thing is, I felt for him too. I couldn't help but wonder if we felt the way we did because it was immediate and tangible. Maybe it wasn't real. I couldn't understand why I still had feelings for him. Why was my heart so warm and my shoulder so cold? In my mind, I rationalized our relationship problems as being infinitely broken but my heart still wanted to embrace him. I made every effort to be good to him. I had a habit of allowing my emotions to take control of me. I would make myself feel better by burdening others with my problems, sharing the weight. I know that wasn't right. That's why I'm not doing it now, but it's difficult dealing with a defunct relationship amidst the loss of my mother and daughter. At first I was mad at him for even bringing it up. I was so flummoxed over this. Sometimes I think he does not deserve me and other times I don't want to live without him. I've never felt such love for anyone that sustained a commensurable amount of frustration. Ideally, I'd love to go back to the day when we were all together and life was filled with hopes and dreams.

I watched him sleep. I tried to stare right into him, into his mind. If only there were a way of penetrating that brain of his and conversing telepathically, answers would be much clearer. If we knew exactly what the other was thinking and could hear those thoughts, there would be no miscommunications or misunderstandings. Then again, sometimes I think it's a blessing not knowing absolutely everything on a man's mind. I'm sure glad he doesn't know everything on mine.

My eyes grew heavy from staring at him and, amidst great struggle, I fell asleep. I began to dream of us. There was a time when in wondering I gazed into the distance of our past and questioned if he ever really knew me. The days of present prove positive he knows me better than he once did. The question now is, gazing forward and inward, deep into my heart and wondering, can he see?

Actions speak louder than words. A picture is worth a thousand of them. Words are cheap and boorish, intangible to the carnal desire of the heart. Great they sound, but like a consommé, they lack any hearty substance, leaving one unsatisfied and looking for more. What is missing from my words when he knows I care for him so deeply, enough for such a strong word to draw from my heart? Love. A dangerous word. His beautiful face etched in my mind and his soul inscribed into my heart, the memories of a time well spent and the possibilities of forthcoming adventures penned across the canvas of my mind's eye.

I ache in the wonder of all that we could be and the possibility of never knowing or exploring those uncharted waters to see what may lie on the other side of the sea. May we find storms so strong or an island with waters so blue, one of such like Fiji or Bora Bora, we can only wonder, but at least that adventure would be with him. One may ask, "Why then, to a woman whom in her heart feels so strongly for the man in which she is wed, why alone would she wish to venture across that sea?" Again I gaze into the distance of wonder, searching for the answers unknown, troubled mind and troubled soul already rocking in the storm. The dark clouds pelt lightning bolts down, bellowing thunder pollutes the night air with its sound and rain cascades from the sky like bullets blazing from a lover's gun. Seas crash around me, attempting to cloak me in their frigid waters. The focus of my mind clouds and sparks like the storm among the seas.

Answers are unknown when questions are unclear; hence the words of my tongue speak not fully of which is my heart. Articulating my love and passion for the man right in front of me, why is that so hard and tortuous to the soul? Is it fear of the unknown, alien territory that lies ahead? A simple life is never given. Choices I am too weak to make. I lie back in the boat and let the sea take me away. No more does my hand carry him by a string or walk him like a dog, spin him around the world or simply draw him to and fro. He thought I saw him as a toy, an inanimate object in which to play with as a child. He doesn't understand what I really see: his rugged beauty, a special uniqueness, a treasure not to be missed and the world to which I am. He speaks of knowing, analytically, the true meaning of the motions of my heart, but the beatings of which are felt for him can only truly be measured by me. They cannot be analyzed from afar, seen with any telescope or measured by some device. Only one device can measure him that is in my soul and that is me.

I hope for the time with him and the answers to why such obstacles position themselves as hurdles in our lanes and hoops in our course. I want to travel toward him with my spirit and see where and if we shall intertwine. My heart is not done with him, yet we turn away. To him it seems simple to just, "cut the rope that holds you down," but for me it is not quite that simple. I could ask him to forgive me for being so afraid of making the wrong choice that I make none. I just continue forward with the wind, sealing the envelope of my fate, but asking a man to forgive such a thing would be impractical.

The least of what I could ask is that he does not falsify or underestimate the feelings in which I hold for him. That may make it harder for him to understand, but if he could travel inside my mind, I know he would.

We turn away and take our steps, pistols positioned at our sides. Count the paces before we turn. One. Two. Three. No need to shoot. It already hurts. In my heart rests the bullet from the moment we turned away.

I cracked my eyes open from my dream, but I think I was still asleep and dreaming when I muttered the words aloud to him, "I love you, too." It was still the middle of the night and dark, as he lied next to me asleep. I'm quite sure he was sleeping and did not hear me because he didn't even flinch and his breathing was heavy like in a dream. It didn't matter. I didn't want him to hear me. I just needed to say it aloud.

I don't remember dreaming anything after that. I don't even recall falling asleep again, but the next thing I noticed, the room was bright and I was in bed alone. The first thing that I think every morning when I awake is always the same. My heart sinks into my stomach when I wake up to realize that Alyssa is gone and it wasn't all just a dream. Every morning the reality hits me like I'm losing her all over again. I can't put into words the way it makes me feel because there are no words powerful enough to describe the excruciating pain that lives within my heart.

Sometimes I can still smell the florid scent of my mother's perfume. Prophetic thinkers claim that when visited by ancestral apparitions, they carry their familiar scent from when they were living. I believe that to be an acceptable explanation, but have not yet accepted the idea that my mother nor Alyssa are gone for good, so I hypothesized my own theory for why I would smell my mother's perfume.

Our brains can remember sights, sounds, tastes and textures, so why then could it not also remember scents? If the memory of a certain scent is so strong and so powerful, and I so desire to smell it once again, then it only seems plausible that we can recall it. I believe that my desire for everything to return to normal, combined with the pain I feel from the loss, causes my brain to provide me with such false sensations as my mother's floral fragrance.

I have really separated myself from my old life, the one I loved. Nothing is the same anymore and it all seemed to change in an instant. I lost my mother and daughter. My dog is gone. I'm living in a completely different home. My husband and I aren't like we used to be. I'm taking a leave of absence from work. My life has almost quite literally turned itself upside-down.

If I can't have it all, if life can't go back to exactly the way it was, why can't I just have something? I suppose I could go back to work by choice, but my mind is too consumed with all that is going on. I couldn't go back so soon. I wanted them to show reruns until I returned. Not knowing how long I would be absent, management thought the best thing to do would be to have someone temporarily take my place. I'm afraid to turn on the TV. My mind floods with curiosities. Who did they get to fill in for me? I have a fear that maybe she's better than me. What if her ratings are higher than mine? I also fear that she's awful. If she doesn't do a good job, the show may lose viewers. My supervisors may resent me for taking a big chunk of time off but maybe they didn't say anything due to the circumstances. I worked so hard for my dream and part of me feels like I'm throwing it all away.

I ask myself, what if Alyssa and mom never return? It's a horrible thought but I can't help but think that's possible. Will I ever go back to work? When is the time right? Should I force myself to work even if I don't want to? Am I doing the right thing by taking the time to let my heart heal at its own pace? These are all questions that I should not be asking myself. I should be discussing them with my husband, the man I loved talking to because he always made me feel better. No matter how I felt about myself, he always had a way of saying the right things. He's very intelligent, very sweet and very caring. It's hard to look beyond the hurt, even though most of it was a lack of communication and misunderstandings.

I'm not quite sure how any of that even matters, if we have construed the meaning of our difficulties to be misunderstandings. We understand that they were just misunderstandings, so letting the past stand in the way couldn't possibly make sense. I told myself that I was going to make a stronger effort this time around, but that's not exactly what I was doing. I was putting a band-aid on a shark bite. If I wanted it to work, I needed to do something drastic.

CHAPTER | 15

JAMES

AT first light I jumped out of bed, threw on the dirty clothes which had littered the floor and slipped out of the house neither showered nor shaven with my hair running rampant, darting away from my scalp like the snakes on Medusa's head. I dashed into Agent VanSlyck's office, greeted by her in a simple manner. I could tell her enthusiasm at such an early hour was not as strong as mine. Not particularly a morning person, her tired mind questioned what had me so anxious. I fumbled in my pocket, reaching for my cell phone. I pulled it out and frantically searched for the pictures as she slowly organized her workspace to prepare for her day. I extended the phone under her face and showed her the picture I took of the basement in that old Victorian home.

At that time, I didn't realize what a useless piece of evidence I held in my hand. She was nice about telling me that, being the sympathetic and softhearted soul that she is. She wasn't there to talk down to me regarding how much more she knew about law than I did, but she was concerned about how I came by that picture and found Mr. Abough in the first place.

The picture I had was not useful as evidence because it proved nothing. He wasn't in the picture. She explained that it could have been any place anywhere and that it was too vague to use as evidence. It was dark, blurry and far away not giving any clear indication as to what it was actually a picture of. It was useful, though, in the sense that we learned more about Mr. Abough and that he still holds some dark secrets beyond what we had already known. He's a man taking illegal pictures of underage girls. He's not dropping those rolls of film off to be developed at the corner drug store. It was his hobby; a very sick one. He was a man who took great pride in the art of photography, perfecting his images, so much so that he had his own photo lab. He could have taken digital images and edited them on the computer, but there was something more intimate to him in touching and smelling the paper in the chemicals, watching the young girls developing right before his eyes.

I imagined that a man who takes that much pride and care into something so sick knows the fine details of print photography. He must also be very sharp on how to make a print of such a disturbing photo and turn it into a unique jigsaw puzzle.

It was becoming clearer to us who the puppeteer was, pulling the strings, using Orpheus as his marionette. It upset me that the picture I took was useless as evidence because anything he had in his lab linking him to Alyssa's abduction had surely been destroyed. Nevertheless, it was a useful to us for we learned that he was still around (not on vacation) and that he most definitely had something to hide. Based on my eyewitness account, Agent VanSlyck visited his photo lab for further inquiry. As suspected, the place was a gutted skeleton by the time they got there to search. He removed every last item from that room.

The investigators talked to the employees in the other offices in the building where the photo lab was, but they never noticed any unusual activity. No one asks questions and tends to mind their own business. Don't ask, don't tell. They hardly ever saw him, if at all, and no one had seen him there for weeks. It was clear that he was used to doing all of his work after dark. It seemed as though he was like a demon, never seen but creating chaos in the shadows. It was time to turn on the lights. It was becoming clear that he was the one who hired Orpheus to throw us off track.

❖

I had gone straight home after meeting with
Agent VanSlyck. I was there for not more than ten
minutes as she quickly dismissed the photograph.
I only told her the location of where I spotted him.
Although she didn't believe my story, she
understood a father's need to chase after his
daughter. She didn't believe that I just so
happened to drive by in the middle of the night,
witnessing him entering into a pink Victorian
house. She knew I had been following him, but she
let it go after a firm warning to watch my step for
my sake, Alyssa's and for the investigation.

Kelly was still in bed when I got home. It was
nice to see that she was finally getting some rest
after so many sleepless nights. As I stood in the
kitchen watching the coffee brew, drip by drip, my
eyes glazed over with a haze as my mind traveled
light years away. I couldn't help but think that I
could have done more. I was so close to him, but I
just let him go. I presumed the picture would be
adequate enough to further the investigation. Part
of me wished that I had just attacked him and beat
him until he took me to where he had Alyssa. The
more I thought about that missed opportunity, the
more I hated myself. Knowing that I was so close,
that we keep getting close, but came back with
nothing was a growing worry in my mind.

I was startled and almost jumped in fright,
before stiffening up, when Kelly's lips pressed

against the back of my neck. I thought she was still in bed.

Her soft warm lips kissed up my neck and to the back of my ear. She put her hands on my waist, turned me around and pushed me into the counter where her lips sank into mine. My mind questioned the reality of the situation and tried to dissect a meaning, but my lips stayed focused. They stayed locked on hers. I was filled with dueling emotions, passion and pain, love and lament.

Her kiss became aggressive as her hands more actively traced my body, then up my shirt to my bare skin. The passion rose and I joined in her intensity. She pulled back her lips for a moment, catching her breath. Her beautiful emerald eyes locked with mine. It was like I was watching her in slow motion, filled with anticipation. She gently parted her lips with a light exhale. She licked her lips with her tongue while taking in a deep breath. She opened her lips and softly she spoke to me, "Will you be my husband again?"

I laughed a breath of happiness as we locked lips once again and continued tearing at each other's clothes. We ripped our clothes off right there in the kitchen. It was the first time we made love since, since, it was the first time since – the first time in a very long time.

Lying together in each other's arms on the cold kitchen floor, she lifted her head off of my chest and spoke, "You never answered my question. So, will you?"

"Will I what?" I asked.

"Will you be my husband again?"

I lifted up my head, looked her in the eyes and said, "I never stopped."

"So that's a yes?"

"Yes."

Life is full of unexpected twists and turns, surprises around every corner, coming at us in every direction. Sometimes they're safe. Sometimes they're catastrophic. That was one of the good ones. It was a moment's distraction, a moment we got caught up in. We needed each other and she was the one strong enough to make the first move. I'm glad she did. So is she. It's the one bit of normalcy we have in our lives. When we have no hope, at least we have each other.

We stopped hearing much from the police and the FBI. I knew they were still trying to find Alyssa, but I guess given the circumstances, it wasn't worth trying to make contact if there was nothing significant to report. I honestly didn't think we would hear from them much at all. Not until the day they knock on the door with Alyssa. Worrying so much and wishing for answers from the police wasn't the best way to keep her alive in our thoughts. Nothing was to be gained by worrying. There was a better way to keep her alive in our hearts and minds, a way without obsessing over the case.

It was Alyssa's birthday. A raging fire burned through my veins, infuriated because there would be no party, cake, or gifts, just the wonders of the mind encircling thoughts of her and praying that she would come home soon. To my surprise, John and Melissa organized a candlelight vigil for Alyssa that night in remembrance of her birthday. It's what I needed to ease my mind.

Just after dinner as the sun began to set around 6 o'clock, friends, neighbors and strangers gathered around, tightly bundled in their winter wardrobe, on that cold evening in March. John, the Master of Ceremonies, did a commendable job in organizing and rallying support. It was touching to see how good people can come together in bad times. Several news trucks showed up, but they were all very respectful. They kept their distance without getting in the way of the ceremonies. I didn't mind this getting on television, even though the media exposure was something we were trying to avoid. I saw no harm in publicizing a candlelight vigil.

John borrowed a sound system from a friend of his who plays acoustic cover songs at the local bars. Sometimes John sings with him. John got up behind the microphone and began the night by speaking to everyone.

In his deep, authoritative voice, John's words boomed into the microphone causing it to screech, "Hello everyone. I just wanna thank you all for coming out tonight. I know it's cold and a little windy so the fact that you came out means all the more to me, Melissa and of course Kelly and James. For those of you that don't know me, I'm John, a long-time friend of the family and Alyssa's Godfather. First, I just have a few things I wanna say, then I'll pass the microphone over to Father Emerson, who will say a few words and a prayer. We not only light candles tonight for Alyssa but also for her grandmother, Kelly's mother, Paige. Both went missing on the same night while she was babysitting Alyssa. Over there you'll find memorials where you may place flowers or candles. We will all be joining together in a song, then going inside where you'll find refreshments. The house is open. If you need to use the bathroom or you find yourself getting too cold, you're welcome to go inside. With that said, I just wanna say, James, Kelly, you have both been very strong through this, much stronger than I'd ever be. I was there when Alyssa was born. Danielle and Alyssa are like sisters and we feel like part of the family is gone. We know she is doing okay though, and in time she will return home. I'd just like to ask everyone to please keep your eyes and ears open and if you see anything or know of anything, please tell someone – Kelly, James, Father Emerson, me or Melissa, the police, whoever you feel comfortable with. Let's just make sure we bring Alyssa home soon. With that, I'll pass it over to Father Emerson."

Father Emerson stepped up to the podium as John stepped down. He addressed the crowd,

"Thank you John. It's every day that acts of evil are in occurrence in this world. It's not every day that they hit home. The most important thing we can remember from today is the love and support of friends and neighbors. It's a love that doesn't end here today, but carries forth in the thoughts and prayers of all of us. It is important that we are there for Kelly and James through all of this and to help them in any way that we can, whether that be big or small. It is important that through all things, we never act alone. All things are possible through the Lord. In hard times such as this, we must put our faith in God. 'Blessed is the man who trusts in the Lord, and whose hope is the Lord. For he shall be like a tree planted by the waters, which spreads out its roots by the river, and will not fear when heat comes, but its leaves will be green, and will not be anxious in the year of drought, nor will cease from yielding fruit.' Jeremiah, chapter seventeen, verses seven and eight. Be like that tree. Spread out your roots to the waters. Be strong. Lean on your friends. Reach out to them. That's why we are here, to help you. Let us now all join in prayer and ask God to watch over Alyssa and Paige."

I didn't realize there was such kindness left in this world. I'm used to witnessing the dark side of human nature. When you work in the news business, you're surrounded by it every single day.

In just one day I could see stories for "Cops Shot," "Hit and Run," "Animal Abuse," "Drive by Shooting," "Child Molestation Charges," "Great Video – Five Dead," and more of the like. I see dozens of news pieces like this a day. Multiply that by five days a week. It started getting to me. I lost all hope for humanity. I didn't watch the news before I started working in it. I hated it for just that reason. It's nothing but bad news. When my daughter was taken and those dark stories became a reality, when we became one of those stories, I was sure there was no hope left. Our friends and neighbors pulled together to prove me wrong. They proved to me that when the going gets tough, humanity does come through. People are there for each other in rough times.

I think as a whole, the human race is generally good. There are a select few that act out and are only self-motivated. Those select few seem to stand out in the crowd which makes them more apparent, when the kind people, who I believe are in the majority in this world, are more humble and blend into the background. They can go unnoticed. When they came out of the background, lit up their candles, sang, prayed and offered us their hope and courage, it restored my faith in humanity.

After spending time with everyone inside the house, discussing the case and talking about Alyssa and Paige, reminiscing on fond memories, people began to dissipate. Eventually, only two remained in the house aside from Kelly and me. They were our two best friends, John and Melissa. They stayed there with us well into the night. It was comforting not having a quiet and lonely house, especially on such a day. It's a day that should have been filled with cake and presents and screaming kids, buzzing toys and loud cartoons on the T.V.

I dream of Alyssa returning home to us and pray that Kelly's mother is safe, but I can't forget to be thankful for the things I do have. Although our dreams may wait in the distance, we must take pleasure in what we have today.

CHAPTER | 16

WHAT becomes of a day when you turn back the clock and motion a life in reverse to glance at something you did not see before? To know then the things I know now, what could have been done differently to prevent the troubles that lay burden in my heart? The night of Alyssa's birthday, the candlelight vigil, if I had only known the truth of it all.

That night, Alyssa sat on a wooden chair in a dimly lit room, wearing a blindfold, or something more resembling a black handkerchief. It was tied tightly around her eyes so she could not see.

"Can I take it off yet?" she asked, as she moved uneasily in the chair, picking at the blindfold.

"Not yet," replied the soft voice in the dark.

Alyssa waited in her chair as we were far away from her, lighting candles and praying for her safety. It was the most we could do at the time. According to Orpheus, she was in an undisclosed location, tied to a chair as in the picture on the puzzle, waiting for us to find her. Without knowing where she is, he was sure we would fail. That's why he was having us play all of those games. He was trying to give us clues as to where she is located, but I don't think he ever knew where to find her. His is just a middleman. The clues were just meant to lead us in the wrong direction.

Regardless of any direction he tried to lead us in, the truth can only be hidden for so long. We came together as a community, as friends, as a family – as one. We held our candles as high as our hopes. Our hopes were to find the truth. Finding the truth would find Alyssa and Paige.

In addition to all the candles we lit for Alyssa and Paige, there was one more candle lit that night. The dim light in the room where Alyssa sat, blindfolded, came from a single flickering candle. With the lights turned out, the number 5 candle atop her birthday cake gave the room an orange glow. The birthday cake was placed down on the kitchen table in front of her, prepared and baked especially for Alyssa by the one who placed it in front of her, the one who took Alyssa.

"Okay. You can take it off now," said Paige.

Alyssa took off the blindfold. Her eyes drew bright and wide when she saw the cake. She shouted with great exclamation, "Cake!"

She blew out her candle and Paige cut the cake. Paige and Alyssa ate the cake together, celebrating her birthday without Kelly and without me.

It was a few days after the candlelight vigil, Agent VanSlyck found the abductor, Alyssa's own grandmother, Kelly's mom, my mother-in-law. She stole our child. It was she who hired Orpheus. I'm still not sure if she sent the package with the lock of hair or if Orpheus did, but him running the show for Paige makes sense since all contact ceased once he was in custody.

Paige was witnessed by an anonymous woman, perhaps an old bingo or Mahjong partner. The witness reported to the police that she was seen alive and well, shopping at the local grocers after the date of her disappearance. She was shopping alone and incognito. Perhaps she was shopping for a birthday cake. I'm not sure if the witness approached her or not. I don't have all the information. I just know she was spotted hiding in plain sight at the grocers when she was supposedly abducted and left for dead.

This discovery brought us from a feeling of disconsolateness to one of puzzlement as we tried to piece together why Paige would hire a man to so elaborately stage a kidnapping of her and her own granddaughter. More important than the question, "Why?" is the question, "Where?"

Upon searching her home a second time, there were no traces that she ever returned after leaving to babysit Alyssa, the same night Kelly got the call that changed our lives.

CHAPTER | 17

James

A perpetual vertigo entrapped my irresolute mind as the world seemed to spin at a dizzying pace, leaving me in the dust. I had no answers regarding our situation because I could not evaluate the circumstances comprehensively enough to pose the appropriate questions. Where would I begin?

When we first learned of the news that Paige abducted Alyssa, we were visited by Special Agent in Charge, Nikki VanSlyck. It was a normal day at first, or what was normal as of late. We woke up like any other day, had breakfast and showered; the usual daily routine. Kelly was busy keeping herself occupied with an exercise video while I was fighting with the toilet. When you live in an old house like this, it seems one thing after the next goes wrong. Just as soon as you fix the leaky sink, the toilet handle gets stuck and it won't stop flushing. The daily routine: Occupying ourselves with mind numbing projects to avoid over thinking and worrying about particular events beyond our control.

I opened the door and saw Agent VanSlyck standing before me. My mind was immediately disoriented with a blending of thoughts, hit all at once. Shock. Surprise. Confusion. Hope. Nervousness. Grief. The thoughts charged through my brain as fast as a bolt of lightning charges through the sky. Why is she here when they've been communicating in secret? Did they find Alyssa? Why isn't Alyssa with her? Is she ok? Did something happen to her? The thoughts raced through my mind, from confusion to hope and fear.

She greeted me and asked to come in. At this point, Kelly had already turned off her workout video and was watching us at the door. She came in and sat us down in the living room. Both of our minds were racing.

"The whole way over here I was trying to come up with the perfect way to break this to you," she said, "but there isn't an easy way. As far as we know right now, Alyssa is okay, but we've learned of her abductor's identity."

"What? That's great news!" I exclaimed.

"Not exactly," she returned.

"I don't understand," Kelly said. "If we know where she is..."

Agent VanSlyck interrupted, "We don't know exactly where, but we know who she's with."

"Well, that's a start," I said.

"Who is he?" Kelly asked.

"She," said Agent VanSlyck, correcting Kelly. "She's your mother."

"What?" Kelly said in confusion.

"I don't understand," I added.

She continued, "I know it sounds strange. Your mother, Paige, she hired Orpheus to stage Alyssa's kidnapping. Meanwhile, she took Alyssa away with her."

"All of this!" I exclaimed as I shook my head in anger, "She put us through all of this! For what? Where are they!?"

"We don't know exactly where."

"How do you know this?" Kelly asked.

"We have a witness who spotted her yesterday in Greencastle, Pennsylvania."

"Who?" Kelly asked.

"She didn't identify herself. We figure it could be anyone, an old friend or relative or someone who just knows the situation from the news and felt the need to report it. Do you know why she would be in Greencastle?"

"I don't even know where that is," Kelly answered.

"No family or friends there?"

"Not that I know of."

"Maybe she went there because she has no ties to it," I added. "She thought we wouldn't find her."

"It seems like the obvious thing to do," Agent VanSlyck returned, "but people seldom go somewhere random. They go somewhere comfortable, somewhere that they feel like they can control the situation."

We sat there and talked as Agent VanSlyck, Kelly and I tried to put together what was going on, but none of it made any sense. Why would she take Alyssa? Why Greencastle? Where is that? At least it was a clue, but it was just as bewildering in a different way.

I spoke to Kelly and tried to be strong for her, but I'm still not sure how she feels. I'm sure whatever I'm feeling, I can multiply that by ten, and then I would only be getting a faint glimpse of what she is going through.

When I first met Paige, I remember she was a very hard woman to please. When Kelly and I started dating, saying that Paige was skeptical of me would be an understatement. I had to prove myself worthy of dating her daughter. It was annoying to me to have to prove myself, but I somewhat understood. Kelly is her only child and she wants what's best for her. Being such a beautiful and successful woman, a lot of men surely would have inappropriate motives. What bothered me most about it is, at what point do you just let go and trust your daughter to make her own decisions? She seemed rather controlling. I could see if Kelly was sixteen, but for her to act so inhospitably toward me over a grown woman was unsettling. Her glacial heart and cold demeanor caused me to have an unfavorable first impression of her. Her unresponsiveness to my existence was seemingly a world without end. I thought she would go on ignoring me forever.

I played the game. I was on my best behavior and tried to please her any way I could. Basically, I was myself. It took a long time. There were a lot of days where I just wanted to give up, but eventually she reformed her narrow-minded intolerance into an acclamatory blessing. She finally realized that Kelly and I were meant to be. I was admittedly resentful of her behavior, although her change in attitude toward me finally won me over in good turn. I never had another issue with her. In fact, sometimes I had a feeling that she favored me over Kelly. The stereotypical mother-in-law hatred never applied to me, once she opened up to me. She came to accept me as part of the family. I was the son she never had.

That is why this situation has me in such utter confusion. What would possess her to do something this extreme? The thing that doesn't add up to me are the puzzle pieces, the demands and the games we were being forced to play. If she wanted to disappear and raise Alyssa by herself, she could have just packed her car and vanished. I guess if she did that, it would have been obvious that she took her. In that sense, hiring a man to stage the kidnapping made sense to throw us off, but it should have ended there.

For me, this was just the beginning. I was going to Greencastle.

CHAPTER | 18

OUR life is only as good as the people who are in it. Melissa and John are our best friends, but to say that they are just our friends would not be giving them enough credit. They are family. With Alyssa being gone, they too are missing a member of their family. They were actively trying to find Alyssa just as much as we were. As we were working with authorities, trying to bring Alyssa home, Melissa and John were working to find her in their own way. They worked with Child Find America, a charity that assists parents of missing children. They created flyers with a picture of Alyssa and distributed them all over town. They sent out pictures through the mail. They did all that they could to raise awareness, hoping for someone to come forward who may have information on Alyssa's whereabouts.

As John spoke to me about the charity he has been working with, I was looking over the brochures he had given me. I was somewhat in a state of shock from the statistics I was reading. I almost wasn't surprised, but I couldn't help but find the numbers frightening. In the most recent study, nearly eight hundred thousand children were reported missing. Two thousand children are reported missing to the FBI each day. Every day two thousand children go missing. I can't help but shake my head. That is a staggering amount and those are just the ones reported to the FBI.

I was also surprised by the fact that most children are basically helpless. We don't realize how little a child actually knows. It is our job to teach them everything that they know and sometimes we come up short. When a missing child is found, it is often hard to reunite them with their parents because so many young children do not know their addresses or telephone numbers. Many don't even know their parents' names. They think your name is mommy or daddy. We spend so much time teaching our children not to talk to strangers and just accept that as being enough. When two thousand kids a day are reported missing to the FBI, we think that telling our children not to talk to strangers is enough to protect them – and I thought the children were the naïve ones.

Maybe it's one of those difficult subjects that we don't want to talk about with our kids, like sex. Who really wants to talk about sex to their adolescent teenager? Who really wants to discuss kidnapping with their toddler? No one. Thus, we circumvent the real issues. Statistically speaking, it is more likely for a child to be kidnapped than to be trapped in a fire; however, every child is taught what to do if they catch fire. I guess talking to a kid about a fire is just easier than talking about abduction.

We tell our children, "Don't take candy from strangers." It is not surprising, though, that most abductors are family members, not strangers. Regardless, if the temptation was unavoidable and an offer of candy did lead to abduction, what then will our children do based on what we taught them? In a study, children were approached by a stranger who pretended his dog was missing and asked for the child to help him look. Though the parents warned never to go with strangers, each of those children went with him.

I guess it's not enough for us to tell our children not to talk to strangers. If they are taken, then what do they do? We didn't tell them that part. I guess I'm angry because no one told me. I should have known better, but I wasn't aware of how commonplace it is for a child to be taken away. Nobody told me what to tell my child to do in the case that she was taken from me. I just know to stop, drop and roll for fire because that's all we talk about.

As mad as I am that my mother-in-law has committed such an abominable act of cruelty against our family, displaying her blackened heart for everyone to see, I at least have the comfort in knowing that Alyssa is safe. Thinking she was with a stranger, I had always assumed the worst. When a stranger abducts a child, the first three hours are critical to the child's safe return. Most children who are abducted by strangers are murdered within the first three hours. I just wonder what something like this does to a child's mental state. We should be striving for innocence ourselves, not taking it away from the youth. I truly think we are not to strive for ignorance, or purposely dwell in a state of stupidity in order to lead a blissful life. With closer examination, I believe it to be true. Innocence is bliss.

I don't know what I would do if I found out that Alyssa was – I can't even think the word as my mind goes blank in order to avoid any dangerous emotions caused by such a term. I don't even want to think about it. I cannot imagine what those parents must feel. I would be paralyzed with misery. I would completely give up on life. No matter how much I ponder it and no matter how hard I try to figure it out, I will never understand why someone would want to take the life of a child.

I guess it should have been obvious from the start, but I never would have expected Paige to take Alyssa away from us. I guess it's true what they say, you never truly know anyone. It's just so hard to trust anyone these days, especially with your own child. I would still trust Melissa and John, though with slight hesitation. They have watched Alyssa for us many times before, but I would surely keep a more watchful eye on her. I guess it's not good to be over protective either. Maybe we did all that we could do. Melissa and John always proved themselves to be trustworthy and Alyssa particularly liked seeing Danielle. Alyssa and Danielle are the same age and are like sisters – even closer because they don't fight like sisters do.

It's great to have friends like them in life. Kelly and I never got out much so we never had the opportunity to make a lot of really close friends. People seem to be too busy for friends these days. Life takes over, especially as you get older. I'm glad that out of all the people in the world, we have become close friends with Melissa and John. They are two of the best friends anyone could possibly ask for. Most people aren't fortunate enough to have people as great as them in their lives. I feel truly blessed to know them.

When I told John the information we had obtained from the FBI about Paige being Alyssa's abductor, his exasperation was much like my own.

He did not understand how someone could purposely create such turmoil within their own family. It's unfathomable how she could just turn her back on the ones who love her. I told him of my plans to take the flyers he created to Greencastle. He asked me for a picture of Paige because, being the great friend that he is, he wanted to create a new flyer for me with her picture on it too.

With all of the stress in life and when struggling through such hard times, I've always tried to swim against the current. I've grown weak, tired. Life doesn't have to be so hard. All I have to do is lay on my back and float. The waves will wash me back to shore. Whenever I take a moment in my life to put down my worries and articulate exactly what I need and why, when I ask it is given. I just have to clearly know what I want, have good intentions for wanting it and sincerely believe that by asking I will receive. By projecting my intentions, my emotions and my energy into the universe – my pure desires will return to me in a positive manner. There must be no doubt, no fear, nor sorrow, only faith and hope.

I need to do that this time, not with worry in my heart as I think the worst. I need to ask and know that I will receive. I need to knock and know that the door will be opened. I need to seek and be positive that I will find her. I will bring her home.

❖

I've never been to Greencastle. I didn't quite know what to expect. To tell you the truth, before this, if you asked me to point it out on the map, I couldn't. It didn't matter though. We had the car packed with three bags and GPS. One bag was filled with Kelly's things and the other with mine. We were planning on staying there awhile. We did not expect to find Alyssa the moment we rolled into town.

The third bag was filled with the leaflets that John made for us. They had both Paige's and Alyssa's pictures side by side. It included a brief description and an 800 number for reporting information. Our plan was to post them all over town, go from shop to shop and door to door and gather all the information that we could. Local police were doing their job in the search, but we didn't want to sit hundreds of miles away just waiting for news.

We set out for Pennsylvania with about a four-hour drive ahead of us. We were splitting the drive in half. Kelly would drive the first two hours and I would drive the rest of the way. When we stopped halfway to switch, we went into a diner for a quick bite to eat. Much like the rest of the New Jersey diners, it was cloned and positioned conveniently off the highway, a giant castle made of mirrors, reflecting the neon rainbows and jewels. There is nothing subtle about the Jersey diners.

As Kelly was in the restroom and I was mulling over the menu, I noticed the payphone by the front door. Being caught up in all of the emotions, the cloudiness of my mind never permitted me to think of what should have been obvious.

As Kelly walked back to the table, before even sitting down, I asked, "Did you ever try calling your mother?"

Kelly shook her head slightly with confusion.

I continued, "All this time we thought your mother was missing, ya know – but now we see that's not true. Call her from the payphone. We just call and find out what's going on."

"She's not gonna answer."

"That's why we call from the payphone, so she doesn't recognize our number."

"I don't know."

"We have nothing to lose. I mean, she's your mother. There's gotta be some kind of, I don't know, something. A mother-daughter bond. You two were very close. Maybe just hearing your voice will snap her back into reality."

Kelly stared up at the payphone for a long time then said, "I'm nervous."

"You talk to millions of people for a living. This is your own mother we're talking about."

"That's different. I don't see or hear those people and so much isn't at stake."

"Just call her. I mean, we're sitting here talking about it. She might not even answer."

"What do I say if she picks up?"

"Talk to her. Find out where she is, how Alyssa's doing and, ya know, how we can all be one big happy family again."

"That's not gonna happen."

"Humor her."

"I think I'm gonna need a few minutes, alone."

Kelly, after much hesitation, stood up and walked over to the phone. I watched her go to the phone and look back at me. She stood there by the phone and the rancid gumball machines, rack of car and apartment publications, and the single payphone. She took some time to collect her thoughts. I returned my eyes to the menu and tried to give her as much privacy as I could.

A young waitress approached me. As Kelly was still by the phone, I ordered for her. I ordered light, two sodas and two sandwiches for Kelly and me. After the waitress took the order and walked away, I glanced over to see how Kelly was doing. She was still standing by the phone, staring at it. I understood. Although I tried to push her into calling, I know that I'd be really nervous about it too. Then again, I didn't really expect Paige to answer a number that she didn't recognize. I didn't expect she'd even have the phone anymore. I just assumed that it would be worth a try.

I sat there and drank my soda as the sandwiches arrived. Before taking a bite from my sandwich, I looked back through the glass double doors again. I was going to wait for her until I began eating, but I wanted to give her time. After I had a few bites out of my sandwich, Kelly walked back to the table.

"Did you call?" I asked.

"I don't have any change," she replied.

"Oh."

"I finally got up the courage to call and then reached in my purse – everything should really take debit cards these days."

Not having any change either, I took a dollar bill out of my pocket and got change from the register. I kept the coins and walked to the payphone with her. I dropped the coins down the slot, dialed the phone, and then handed it to her.

"I'll leave you alone in case she answers," I said.

I walked away and headed back to my sandwich. As I approached the table to sit down in front of my meal, my cell phone rang. I pulled it out of my pocket and answered. I found it odd and was slightly confused that right after I dialed the payphone for Kelly, my phone rang. For a moment, I thought I called myself by mistake.

"Hello?"

"James?" asked a female's voice.

"Yes?"

"This is Agent VanSlyck."

"Oh. How are you?"

"Okay. How's everything?"

"Well, ya know."

"Yeah. Listen, I'm calling because we might be able to make a little progress here but we need your help."

I glanced back to Kelly again to see her coming back from the phone. That was too fast. I knew she must not have gotten in touch with Paige.

Agent VanSlyck continued, "He said he wants to make a confession but will only go on record with you. He wants to meet with you."

"Is that a good idea?"

"If you're not comfortable, that's fine, but he's willing to confess to you. We might find out where she is."

It didn't take a lot convincing for me to go along with that. If it took sitting down face to face with him, that's what I was prepared to do to get my daughter back. Kelly caught the tail end of my conversation and we both realized our route would be diverted back home and away from Greencastle. It didn't matter. We both felt that it was the better thing to do. We were blindly driving into town with nothing to go on. By talking to Orpheus, we thought that we might be able to get the exact address. Two steps forward and one step back, but at least we were still one step ahead.

CHAPTER | 19

Orpheus

It was just a job. I don't judge them for what they are. If the price is right, what do I care? We all need to make a living. Some guy she knows somehow knows someone who knows me. We arranged a meeting, met at the food court in the mall. She sat at the table next to me. We ate, pretending not to know or be talking to each other, but we did. There we discussed all the plans to kidnap your daughter, over chili cheese dogs and a sandwich. I was never involved with a kidnapping before, but like I said, if the price is right. It wasn't hard. She acted as if she was playing some sort of game with your daughter, taking all kinds of pictures and stuff, playing dress-up. Eventually, she proposed the picture of her tied to the chair right before a picture of pretending to be the Statue of Liberty and right after pretending to be a caged animal in the zoo. She made it so your daughter was not afraid. I personally found it to be pretty strange and disturbing, but she was paying me so I did what she wanted.

She didn't know how to use a camera, so she introduced me to your daughter as a friend. I just snapped the shots. I didn't get involved. Like I said, I don't judge.

She told your daughter that you and your wife were on a vacation. You took a cruise or something and will be gone for a long time. She helped her pack a bag of her own as she explained it would be a fun time for them to take a trip too. She put your daughter and her suitcase in the car and fastened her into the back seat, making sure the child locks were on. She opened the door to the front seat, put the key in the ignition and turned on the car. Then she put the radio on, nice and loud. She explained that she had to go inside to get her bag, then she'd be back and they could be on their way. That's when she closed the car door, went back inside and shut the garage door behind her. She called your wife from the house phone, and then it began.

She dialed your phone number. I just started smashing up anything in sight as she sat there and watched, screaming for dramatic effect. We made a lot of noise, but there's no way your daughter heard. You got a real big home. We were all the way on the other side and she was in the car, in the garage with the doors closed and the radio on.

After about five minutes, I disconnected the phone. She grabbed her suitcase and was off with your daughter. I knew I only had a few minutes to get myself out of there because I'm sure you called the police. I smashed up as much as I could on my way out, but all the smashing must have scared the dog. Big mad dog. He came at me. I had no choice.

This seemed like it was going to be a relatively easy job. The hardest part was over. All I had to do now was get the puzzle and put it on your doorstep. I have a friend, Evan, who has a private photo lab. He owed me a favor. I went that night to some basement where he does all his work. He has his own darkroom where he develops his photos, found a way to develop a picture and make a real puzzle out of it. He did all the work in one night as I waited. Just before daybreak, I put the puzzle on your steps and went home to bed. It was a long, tiring day.

I watched your house, drove by now and again, parked down the street and then at one point, you left. As soon as you got out of your car at the post office, I put the note on your window. I had prerecorded the message that you called while I sat, bored in front of your house. I went to the bus stop, but I didn't stay. Shortly after I dropped the package on the bench, I saw some cops roll up so I left. The ten thousand dollars was supposed to be part of my payment. She gave me half up front, the ten from you was a bonus to keep me going and the second half was to be from her once it was over. I've been holding out for my second half to make this all worth my while, but I don't want it anymore. I just want this to all be over. I never thought it was going to get this complicated. As I said, I've never been involved with a kidnapping before. I still haven't, because I don't have your daughter. I didn't take her.

I've done some bad things. I've been to prison before. I've stolen and I've robbed. I even hurt some people real bad, but I never killed anyone and I don't want to be known as a kidnapper – not of a child – not anyone. I broke your stuff. I killed your dog. I mislead the investigation. I don't know if that makes me an accessory, but I didn't do it. I didn't take your daughter.

I wish I could tell you where she is. I know you see me as some kind of monster, not the caring person that I really am, but I do have feelings. I didn't think about what I was doing and how it would affect your family. As I said, it was just a job. I never wanted to harm anyone. Seeing all the pain this has caused you, your family, even the whole community, that's why I decided to speak. The money I was holding out for, it's not worth it.

There's not a lot of information I can give you. She didn't say where she was going or for how long. Once she got in her car, that was the last I saw or heard from her. That's how she said it would be until the job was over, and then she would contact me for final payment. To me, I thought it was a strange reason, but what did I care? She paid cash, and a lot of it. She told me my job would be over once you and your wife worked out your differences and got back together. Once you and your wife got back together, she was going to let herself be found, as if she were a victim too, who was kidnapped along with your daughter. She didn't want her grandchild being passed between homes or in the middle of fights during a separation so she took her to raise her on her own. That is, until you two could work it out. I'm not one to get involved anyone's personal lives, especially those who I work for. Turns out, this job I was specifically hired to do just that.

I know I shot at you, but I was scared. I didn't think you were going to be so aggressive toward me like that. I had to come up with something to scare you. I didn't know the FBI was going to shoot back. I didn't know they were there. I guess it was stupidity on my part. I thought I scared you into having no police contact, but obviously, I was wrong. I never meant what I said about harming your daughter. I couldn't. I'd never harm a child, but it didn't matter. I didn't want to. I just wanted to scare you. It was her idea. She said, the more I scared you both, the more you would need each other for comfort. So, the more I scared you, the better chance I had at getting paid. It was part of my job to monitor you and alert her if I saw any signs of you and your wife working things out.

❖

James

I stood up from the table as Orpheus finished his sentence and, without saying a word, walked to the door. A look of confusion sculpted itself on his face when I left during his confession. I'm not sure if he was finished or not.

I brought myself to the opposite side of the two-way mirror where Agent Spencer and Agent VanSlyck looked in on the confession.

"Does she know he's here?" I asked.

"Not unless he told her," replied Agent VanSlyck. "As you know, for the safety of your daughter, we haven't been releasing any information about the case."

"So, if he's telling the truth and she did hire him and there's no one else involved, as far as she knows, he's still out there and she's still waiting for information?"

"Most likely."

"Let's use that, give her what she wants, bait her in and get my daughter back."

CHAPTER | 20

THE sun was an emphatic light in the sky, pushing away the clouds on each side and revealing the blue canvas beneath. It was a blank canvas, one in which I was ready to paint the future on. In my mind, I already illustrated us beneath the blue sky living out our lives in peace. Sometimes I admit to the dangers of planning for a future. It's both seemingly a blessing and a curse to be aware of time, particularly, the past and the future, when so much of what we have been witness to can haunt us, and our plans for the future could deteriorate. I don't hold on to the pain of losing Alyssa and all that we went through. I let that pain float away with the clouds. I don't hold any grievances in my heart. Orpheus is just a thug, like any other, who moved pieces around in the game for money. Evan Abough was part of the game, after all, though not as big of a part as we had originally thought. He just put together the jigsaw puzzle in his secret photo lab. His bigger crime laid elsewhere in child pornography. I can only be thankful, if I'm going to count my blessings, that Alyssa was not a part of that.

Paige played the biggest role in this whole scheme. She was the one who perpetuated evil and pain throughout our family and community. Kelly and I have forgiven Paige for what she has done. We do not have any resentment in our hearts toward her; however, one must understand that forgiveness does not mean everything can go back to normal (one big happy family). Trust and forgiveness are two separate things, especially when it comes to the welfare of a child.

"The wise are cautious and avoid danger; fools plunge ahead with reckless confidence." -Proverbs 14:16.

We went ahead with my plan. Agent Spencer became the mastermind of the operation, coordinating pictures and information to send to Paige via Orpheus. For his alliance, he was charged with less of a crime. It was still numerous, from breaking an entering to animal cruelty to child endangerment; they threw everything in the book at him except for the kidnapping. That was the deal. He would cooperate if not charged for being an accessory to kidnapping. As I said, I just wanted my daughter back. I wasn't out to punish anyone. Revenge means nothing if I don't have Alyssa.

We made the deal and he told us how to contact her. Paige gave Orpheus an email address at the start and instructed him to send any information to that address. We also obtained access to his email account so when the message was sent, it was from the email address that she was expecting. We wanted it to go smoothly with no surprises.

Agent Spencer snapped some photographs of us. Although they were staged, they appeared as though they were surveillance photos taken by Orpheus. He shot them from a distance, through trees and bushes, behind garbage cans, through windows, anywhere that looked like he was hiding. We just walked through town holding hands, kissing, hugging and he snapped photographs of us. That was hard evidence to prove to Paige that Kelly and I are back together, straight from the horse's mouth: Orpheus (or so she would think).

Agent Spencer's email was convincing, as were the photographs. He wrote a detailed note about our progress, pretending to be Orpheus, and attached several of the photographs to the email. She sent a reply email to Orpheus, unknowingly revealing all the information to Agent Spencer.

Paige Cunningham
To: Orpheus Dunedin

This is wonderful news! I was not expecting to hear from you, especially so quickly, but that didn't stop me from checking my email every day. Leave them a note with the address indicating where they can find us. When they find Alyssa and me, we'll both be as if we were your victims so they will never know I was part of this. And no worries for you. Because you never revealed your identity, when they question me, I will tell them that we were blindfolded and never got a look. I won't give them any information. Once I am able to, I will transfer the rest of the funds into your account. Here is the address we can be found at. Be sure to get this to them ASAP: 15245 Wishing Rock Road, Shady Grove PA 17256.

We learned a lot from a seemingly simple email. The email confirmed the reason why Orpheus did not want to speak at first, in promise of additional funds upon completion of the job. We also learned that she was in Shady Grove, which is in Antrim Township, just outside of Greencastle. Her email response was good evidence to charge her, but the only thing that I was concerned about

was that address.   I was ready to bring Alyssa
home.

As anxious as Kelly and I were, the police
instructed us that we will not be allowed to go into
the house to get our daughter.   The police would
have to go in themselves and secure the area, then
bring Alyssa out to us.

The Pennsylvania State Police were alerted
immediately after the email was received.   They
wasted no time.   The FBI briefed the state police on
the situation in great detail and instructed them on
what to do.   Shady Grove was nearly four hours
away from us.   We all wanted Alyssa brought to
safety immediately and did not want her there for
four hours longer than she had to be.   We got into
the car with Agent Spencer and he drove us to
Shady Grove as the Pennsylvania State Police
prepared to get Alyssa.   We were going to meet her
at the police station.

The state police drove down the long, straight
and flat road surrounded by farmland on an
unseasonably warm and sunny afternoon as the
first day of spring approached.   They turned off the
road and headed down a long and dirt driveway.
With a dusty cloud behind their wheels, they
ambulated down the rocky path to the old white

farmhouse. The paint was chipping off its wood, exposing the weathered siding covered with mildew. The grass was burnt to a dry brown and clouds of dusty dirt blew in the wind. It was as though this house has been overlooked for half a century.

The cars stopped by the house and the officers grouped at the edge of the driveway. They made their way up the walk to the rickety old porch. They tried to walk quietly, though the impressions on the wood squeaked as their boots sounded like thunder. Without much force, the door broke open with the first blow as if it had disintegrated off its hinges. Like skilled veterans, they entered the house with guns drawn, covering each other for protection. The house was practically empty. Few signs of life were visible, similar to an abandoned home with uninvited guests. The house was covered in dust and dirt. Several windows were broken and boarded up and the staircase to the upstairs level looked like it would collapse with a good hard sneeze. The house showed signs of recent activity though, such as a couple of dishes on the table and a half filled bag of garbage on the floor.

The police continued through the home and searched carefully within all the rooms. In an upstairs bedroom, they found a child's sleeping bag on the dirty floor. In the same room was a dusty green sofa with the cushions so worn they practically sunk through the bottom. On top of it laid a light sheet and a pillow, suspected where Paige stayed with Alyssa. By the looks of the home, it was obviously not sustainable for them. If Paige was truly checking her email every day, she must have made her way into town at least once a day without being recognized, until the fateful day when she was spotted by the anonymous witness.

The last room in the house left unchecked was the basement. No light was available at the flick of a switch so police carefully descended the steep, wooden, ladder-like stairs to the musty basement. They flashed their lights around and saw a slew of spiders, a dead mouse and a collection of cobwebs, but that was it. No one was in the home. It was uninhabited.

"No one down here!" shouted Officer Trace, a tall and rough looking man with slick dark hair and a moustache.

Officer Trace took another look around the basement, but it was obvious that Paige and Alyssa were not down there. The room was completely desolate. Nothing stored, not even boxes. The only things there cobwebs and dust. If Paige and Alyssa were there, they would have been in plain sight. Officer Trace then caught a glimpse of sunlight in the corner of his eye and turned his attention out the small rectangular window.

"In the shed!" he exclaimed to the men upstairs. "There's a shed in the back!"

The men upstairs quickly made their way to the backyard, all the while, Kelly and I were riding in the car (the longest four-hour car ride in my life) waiting to hear any bit of news from Shady Grove. The longer we rode in the silent car, the more times

I counted the rubber tires thumping on the pavement and the crazier I became. I don't know if it was motion sickness, the hot sun intensifying through the windowpane, the fear and anticipation, or maybe any combination of these, but I felt sick to my stomach and every second dragged on like a minute and every minute felt like an hour. I calculated that in my head and if every minute felt like an hour, it would seem like another 180 days before we got there.

CHAPTER | 21

THE officers made their way across the burnt, dried up grass and dirt toward the broken down old shed. Paige and Alyssa sat in a dark corner in a pile of straw. They were blindfolded, gagged and handcuffed together.

The police approached the shed. Officer Trace looked at the doors, then at the officers behind him. He grabbed the handle and pulled on the door. The wood was warped and scraping on the ground so he put more strength into it, giving it one good tug to open it. The door scraped along the dirt as termites fell out of the wood and scurried all around. Officer Trace became startled and stepped back from the termites. The officers behind him entered the shed with their flashlights to find it completely empty with the exception of a few rusty tools hanging on the wall.

"Looks like this isn't gonna be as easy as we thought," said Officer Trace.

"Let's divide up into teams," called out the elder leading officer. "Grid search the entire farm 'til we find 'em."

The leading officer divided them into two groups and sectioned off the farm into grids. A search grid allows a quick and thorough examination of the grounds. By each team assigned to particular sections of land, searching in a weaving pattern and intersecting one another, every piece of land will be in somebody's line of sight. If something is there to be found, searching in this manner would track it down quickly and increase the likelihood of it being found.

There wasn't a lot to be found. The abandoned farm left not much more than unattended land and tall grass and weeds in the way. They weren't sure what they would find. Their first expectations were that they would easily locate Alyssa and Paige in the house, but it seems Paige was going for a little more authenticity.

From what I've seen on the news, missing persons can even be found buried in a hole in the ground – a large ditch, usually locked and covered with dirt and leaves. They planned to search every blade of grass on that farm. They weren't expecting it to be that difficult. They thought they would find them in the house and call it a day, but more often than not, life gives us what we least expect.

As they ascended the hill, something attracted their attention. In the distance, falling apart just like everything else on the property, there was an old barn with its red paint bleeding off its bone. One group made their way to the barn as the other group continued searching the grounds.

The team approached the entrance to the barn and noticed the door was already open enough to squeeze in. They turned sideways and slid through the door. Sharp beams of sunlight snuck in from the roof, through the broken and weathered wood, into the otherwise dark barn. The officers used their flashlights to look around, seeing much of the same: an abandoned farm. Empty stalls and straw were laid about; however, one officer, Officer Sarah Worthington, noticed something suspicious. She noticed a long wooden ladder on the ground. She tilted her flashlight upward and saw a loft. When the light shined into the loft, she caught a faint glimpse of a figure in the corner and heard a muffled cry for help.

The officers hurried over to the ladder and together they hoisted it up and leaned it against the loft. She gave her flashlight to a fellow officer and they all shined their lights up into the loft as she climbed the ladder. As she reached the top, she saw Paige and Alyssa sitting in a dirty pile of straw, wearing the blindfolds, handcuffs and gags. Sarah climbed into the loft and took the blindfold and gag off of Alyssa as Officer Trace, climbed the ladder.

"You okay, hun?" asked Sarah.

"We're playing hide and seek," Alyssa answered.

"Who you hiding from?"

Trace climbed into the loft. "Everyone okay?" he asked.

He removed the gag and blindfold from Paige and asked, "Where's the key to the cuffs?"

"He has them," Paige replied.

"Who?"

"The man. The one who brought us here."

"Ma'am," added Sarah, "We know. Where are the keys?"

"I don't know what you're talking about."

Alyssa looked on at the officers, getting increasingly more frightened, realizing that this was not just a game. Sarah noticed Alyssa getting nervous so she hesitated for a moment. Trace took out his handcuff keys and removed the cuffs that were binding Alyssa and Paige together. Trace looked at Sarah then got the cuffs free from both Alyssa's and Paige's hands. He carried Alyssa down the ladder while another officer on the bottom held it steady. One of the officers reached out his arms and took Alyssa from Trace so he could more easily climb down the ladder.

Still on the loft, Sarah leaned in to Paige and in a calm and matter-of-fact tone said, "You have the right to remain silent. Anything you say can and will be used against you in a court of law. You have the right to an attorney. If you cannot afford an attorney, one will be appointed to you. Do you understand each of these rights I have explained to you?"

"Yes," Paige replied. "Am I under arrest?"

"Yes, you are."

Sarah waited until Alyssa was escorted out of the barn by Officer Trace and then instructed Paige to climb down the ladder. Sarah followed behind her as an officer waited for her at the bottom. Once Paige reached the ground, he cuffed her hands behind her back.

The officers took both Paige and Alyssa back to the station in separate cars. We were still nearly two hours away from Shady Grove, wishing we were there for her. Alyssa was encumbered with fear, already missing us and then taken from her grandmother as she rode anxiously in the police car with strangers. She thought she had done something wrong for being taken away by the police. She was too young to understand what was really happening.

I think Kelly and I rode just as anxiously as Alyssa did while we sat in the car with Agent Spencer. Our drive felt like an everlasting stretch of pavement, growing longer faster.

I was excited to see Alyssa, but I was also concerned about how she was and what we would say once we saw her. I wasn't sure if I wanted to see Paige ever again.

CHAPTER | 22

THE moment I saw Alyssa wasn't exactly how I pictured it. I envisioned walking away in slow motion from a burning building, carrying her in my arms, with her arms wrapped around my neck and dirt on our faces. I pictured myself carrying her from that blazing building after a big action sequence, fighting off bad guys and navigating my way through dark corridors. I was going to save her, set the place on fire and safely walk out with the bad guys burning behind me. Yeah, that's what heroes do.

The fact is, I was just riding in a car the whole time. I picked her up from the police station in the middle of the afternoon and the bad guys were really just one aging grandma who is indirectly related to me. It's not what I pictured at all. Who was the hero? Was it the police for their infiltration of the farm? Was it the FBI for cracking the case? Maybe it was me for helping put all the pieces together? It could have been Kelly for keeping her sanity and working to get her daughter back. Was it John and Melissa working with the charity to help find her whereabouts? In actuality, I think the real hero in this situation was Alyssa. It's a cruel world we live in and it will try to break us down, but she's strong. She doesn't even let it phase her. We can't let bad people or bad situations get the best of us. If we let it get to us, we let them win – the hard times, the bad people, the pain or the stress – by giving it our attention, we lose the fight. A real hero is someone who can rise above in good spirits and not let it bring them down, and that's exactly what Alyssa did.

She is young and naïve. Much of what has happened to her she most likely didn't even understand. It will probably be buried in her subconscious when she's older, but she's still a hero in my book. She's going to be strong. She's going to grow up and take on this world. This world has big plans for her and no matter what, I know she will be doing something great.

Kelly and I went back and forth in a discussion before we saw Alyssa again, neither one of us holding too firmly to any ideas. We didn't know how to approach this situation. How would we explain to her what really happened? Should we? What do we say happened to grandma when she goes away? How do you explain all of this to a 5-year-old? I thought back to when I was a child. I grew up without my parents, raised by my grandparents. My curious little mind knew something was askew with my life, but as a child, you accept the world around you for what it is, ignorant to the fact that you are really just living in complacency. It took me a long time to find out that my mother was dead. It took a long time before I knew I had a dad, that Grandma and Grandpa were really my Mom's parents, not mine. Still, to this day, I am confused about events from my childhood that were never explained to me. Maybe kids aren't as naïve as we think.

We were escorted into a room where Alyssa was sitting on the floor, playing with another little girl her age while Officer Sarah supervised them. The moment Alyssa saw us come through the door, she jumped up and ran over to us. I scooped her up and Kelly and I hugged her at the same time. She gasped as she ran over, but we were all so speechless. If she had questions at that moment, she didn't ask any of them. Kelly and I were too busy trying to hold back our tears. We tried to keep our composure for Alyssa. Kelly's eyes turned red and welled with tears, but she kept her composure. We were all speechless. Sometimes feelings are much stronger than words. A hug or a gesture, even the energy of love passed through one another, words could ruin that. What mainly hit me is the reality of touching her again. I was hugging my daughter. For so long, I started thinking I'd never see her again. Even though I told myself I would, sometimes it feels like we are just telling ourselves that because we know we need to think positively, but that's not what we really think. Holding her seemed like more of a dream come true than I had ever imagined.

Kelly stayed in the room with Alyssa and let her play with her new friend, Sarah's daughter, as I sat with Paige in another room. That answered any questions that I had about how Kelly felt about her mother. She didn't want to see her. Not yet. Maybe never. I wasn't sure, but I knew that she resented her.

Alyssa was getting pretty anxious, too. She would play for a minute, and then ask Kelly if we could go home. Kelly would tell her, "Not yet," but a minute later, she'd ask again.

I didn't plan on spending much time with Paige. I just felt that I had to see her before we left. We sat in silence for a long time, not knowing what to say to each other. There wasn't much to say. She already knew this could happen. She thought she had a chance to get away with it, but deep down inside, I think she was more expecting this outcome. She seemed to accept it.

I had nothing to say to her. Getting angry or being loud and abusive with my words wouldn't have helped any. I wouldn't have felt good about myself, having to lower myself to that level, allowing my anger to control me. I knew I would feel better walking out of there, knowing I was the better person, rather than saying things just to be hurtful. I had forgiven her because I didn't want to carry that weight in my heart. By giving her my forgiveness, I was able to leave my pain right there in that room.

I just said one thing to her before I walked out, "Every day children are taken suddenly from the world they know into a strange place, forced to live in unfamiliar and frightening surroundings, captive against their will. Now you get to see what that's like."

She spoke no words in return. I spoke none further. I stood up and left the room. I gave her something to think about before she went away to sit confined in a locked cell, and that felt much better than getting angry.

When I returned the room, Kelly didn't ask me any questions. She didn't ask what was said, not by her mother or me. She was ready to leave and so was Alyssa. Although she tried, Kelly hasn't yet forgiven her mother and, even if she had, I know she still wouldn't care about her. I don't think it was this one event that caused her to turn her back on Paige. Even though this would have been enough, there were deeper issues, things I know they never brought up. When things like that pile up, something like this can make you walk away from the relationship without even batting an eye. This alone was enough, but there was so much more.

Alyssa, Kelly and I got into Agent Spencer's car and he drove us home, another eternal car ride with exhaustion. We slept most of the way. Paige was escorted in another car to what would eventually become her new residence. Kelly and I were left with the monumental task of repairing our lives and relationships.

CHAPTER | 23

KELLY and I never used to have a lot of time. We would always see each other in passing and we were usually angry when we did finally spend time together. Our main goal was to move away from that lifestyle. We were lazy when it came to our relationship with each other and our family. We made more time for work and we let our anger get in the way of enjoying and building our relationship. I was envious any time I saw a happy family enjoying their time together, knowing I didn't have that for myself. Both of us, being very unhappy with each other, began to lustfully notice other people. Kelly was greedy for wanting to work so much that she could hardly spare the time for Alyssa and me but at least we had a nice house and she had her face on television screens across the country. I think that plays into pride too. We were a mess.

Kelly and I wanted to move away from all of that. This is not our second chance. That was after Alyssa had gotten sick. This is our third chance. That's why this time we vowed to do it right, first by taking our vows seriously. A promise to God and to each other, in sickness and in health, for better or for worse until death do us part. We need to honor that. We need to not be lazy about working things out when they're bad and we especially can't get lazy about keeping things good. We have to stop envying others for what we don't have. If all we want is a little more time together, we have to just do what it takes to make that time and stop being so greedy about work.

The money and the fame became a lot less important to Kelly once she realized how important family is and especially how delicate the things we often take for granted can be. She never went back to work. Not for the news, anyway. I didn't either. It was too demanding on our family. We sold our old home and put that money in the bank. I've continued fixing up my grandmother's house. That's where we live now. That was already big enough for the three of us. We don't need anything excessive. Kelly decided to go back to school to be a teacher. Her heart just wasn't into her work anymore. She felt she could make more of an impact in people's lives, especially children, as a teacher working with them face to face, not as a picture on the screens across America.

I just needed enough to get by. Like I said, what matters most to me is that I'm home by six for dinner and have enough time to play with Alyssa before the sun goes down. No longer do Kelly and I ever let the sun go down on our anger. We work to bring as much joy as possible into our lives. I've always been handy around the house, but working in home repair has never been my lifelong dream. I never thought it would bring me so much pleasure, but it does. I've never known such joy in my life until now. Even if I was doing what I like, being a cameraman, it brought me no joy when it took me away from my family. Now I have the time for the things that are truly important to me.

I know life now isn't perfect. The road to perfection only leads to destruction. Nothing will ever be perfect. What matters most is making sure you find the time for the things you love – the ones you love. No extraneous factor or material item will transcend our lives into perfection.

Alyssa is enjoying the summer, but I'm not sure how she feels about starting kindergarten. She seems excited about the adventure, but I thought she'd be scared. That little girl has a fire inside of her, ready to take on the world, five years old but so grown up. I have no idea how I felt on my first day of school. I don't remember feeling anything. I don't remember being excited or scared. I was just going with the flow, but that's always been me. I just roll with the punches. I think Alyssa got a lot of her traits from Kelly. That passion and spunk is definitely from her mother.

She doesn't seem to be phased by what happened. Once a week we still talk to a family therapist just to make sure there are no deeply rooted issues. For the last few months there really hasn't been much left to discuss. Alyssa understands what happened and she feels safe now. She never felt bad about it, maybe just confused. Everything seems fine now, though. I'm not saying we're a perfect family. No one will ever be perfect. You'd have quite a complex if you always ran around looking for perfection in your life. We're happy and that's what's important. We have real joy in our lives now. Kelly is enjoying her new career choice. I am happy with mine and we are all glad to be spending quality time together, building a strong family – something we should have done years ago.

John and Melissa come by often with Danielle. Alyssa and Danielle were really excited to see each other again. John and Melissa were excited to see them together again, too. We all were. They are like sisters. John and I are like brothers. I don't know how that works. Maybe Alyssa and Danielle are more like cousins. My point is, we are all very close.

Father Emerson received a very large anonymous donation for the church from us when we sold our old house. I'm sure he knows it was from us, but I prefer not to give my gifts for the recognition. We gave the church the money out of the goodness of our hearts for all he's done to help bring our family back together. He's not only our Priest that we see every Sunday now, but he's become a true friend.

Agent VanSlyck and Agent Spencer are, unfortunately, looking for another child now, I'm sure. I say unfortunately because of the very nature of their work. It's a sad world we live in where that is a job that needs to be done. Whoever they are in search of, their families should have some hope, having such talented and passionate people working with them.

Orpheus Dunedin sits in prison on a twelve-year sentence. Though promised otherwise, he was convicted for carefully planning the abduction and demanding a ransom, the ten thousand dollars he was trying to get from me.

Evan Abough went away for a second time. First, for the statutory rape charges because of having sex with his underage students and now he is serving time in prison for the child pornography obsession he kept a secret for only so long, and a consecutive sentence for child endangerment as an accessory for knowingly participating in the kidnapping conspiracy with Orpheus and Paige.

Well, what about Paige? I didn't mention her for a reason. She is still in prison and out of our lives.

Although it was some time after the fact, we didn't want this to be the only year we didn't celebrate Alyssa's birthday. We had a birthday party for her and, for us adults, it paralleled as a welcome home party as well. Friends and supporters from the community joined us for the occasion and made it her biggest, happiest and most memorable birthday to date. It was like a birthday in the most literal sense, as though we were given the gift of life once more, a rebirth, her first birthday home again. We celebrated our new life together.

I have to admit, I was rather nervous with so many people around. It was hard for me to leave her alone for one second, even though we were in our own home. I didn't want to take my eyes off of her. It's going to take some time for me to get over that. I was protective of her to begin with. I have to be very careful not to ruin her life when she becomes interested in boys. I cannot suffocate her with my paranoia.

Aside from that brief moment of panic, when I realized at some point I had to take my eyes off of her, I had a blast. It was an instinctual reaction. If you've ever felt that sinking feeling in your stomach when you look down and realize your child is not standing next to you as you thought, but then you turn around and there she is, that's the feeling that I had. It was a moment, ever so brief.

She had pizza, unwrapped all of her presents, stuffed her face with ice cream and cake, ran around like a sugar monster with her friends screaming and had a blast, just as she was supposed to. It didn't phase her that it was a late party. She was just having fun. I think I might need to build an addition on the house just to store all of the gifts everyone got her, from crayons to toys and teddy bears and dolls; however, there was one gift that I saved until last. I wanted to wait until a moment when it was just the two of us.

I handed her the poorly wrapped gift that I wrapped myself. She tore it open without noticing my sub-par wrapping job and "oooo-ed" like she was watching the Fourth of July fireworks. She was mesmerized by the colors.

"Do you know what that is?" I asked her.

"A bird!"

"Yeah, it's a bird, but what else?"

"A parrot?"

"Very good, sweetie. It's a kite."

"Oh!"

"Remember you wanted to fly a kite?"

"Can we fly it now?"

"Yeah. Yeah, we can fly it now. We have to put it together first though. Wanna help?"

"Okay."

I opened the package and together she and I figured out how to assemble the kite. Once it was all set up, I put it on the ground and got it ready for takeoff. I handed her the string.

"Now hold on tight. You ready? It's gonna go up in the air."

She threw the reel of string down on the ground but didn't say anything.

"What's wrong?"

"I don't wanna go in the air."

Trying to hold in my laughter, I said, "You're not, sweetie. Just the kite. The kite goes up in the air. Want me to show you?"

"Yeah."

"Here. Watch."

I picked up the kite and the string. I tossed the kite into the breeze and let it fly into the air. She smiled and giggled as the bird caught the wind.

"Should I let him go higher?"

"Yeah!"

I let the string loose and let him fly high in the air.

"Look at 'em go!" I exclaimed.

"Don't let 'em fly away! I wanna try!"

"Okay. Lemme bring him back down and you can try."

I reeled the string back around the spool and drew the parrot closer to us. As it got closer, the kite dove nose first into the ground.

"You broke him!"

"No. He landed. We'll put him back in the air. Take the string."

Alyssa took the string from me and I walked over to the kite.

"You ready?"

"Yeah!"

"Okay, here he goes!"

I threw the kite into the air and it caught the wind. Her face lit up when she saw the kite up in the air and that she was flying it. She was flying a bird. The beautiful colors of the red, blue and yellow parrot danced along the purple sky, reflecting the warming orange of the setting sun.

I walked behind Alyssa and knelt down. I wrapped my arms around her, put my hands on her hands and guided them on the spool of string.

"Watch. Wanna make him go higher?"

"Yeah."

I helped her unravel the string and watched the bird soar higher into the sky. At that moment, I felt safe, like the worst was behind us. It wasn't a white dove, but the parrot still gave me peace in knowing that we were going to be okay. From then on, everything seemed to just work out fortuitously with little to no effort. Naturally, everything fell into place.

I realized that life is filled with moments of joy and moments of sorrow. Our lives are either good or bad, depending on what we choose to remember. I choose to remember the good times. I choose to remember this.

<u>ACKNOWLEDGEMENTS</u>

I am first indebted to God for He has been the source of all creativity and inspiration. For those who have purchased and/or read this book, you are owed great thanks. It is for you that I write. My dreams are that I have given you something that you enjoyed to read. I would like to thank Kristin Holzer for the amazing cover art. I thank all of my family and friends for being so supportive and encouraging, especially my parents Edward and Eileen Keeney. To Margaret Shea, Lillian Ryan, Jennifer McCarthy, Danielle McCarthy, Cody McCarthy, Kristen and John King, Brenda Mosley, Diane Shapley-Box, the Hundertpfunds, and to the rest of my family and friends – their continued love, encouragement and support has been vital through all of my creative works, including this book. I would like to thank (in alphabetical order) Kimberly Applegate, Jerzy Jung, Lena Lyons, Sarael Martinez, Arnold A. Sidney Jr., Anlynn Truong, Shyann Williams, Gregory Robert Wilson, Sharon Zevitt and George Zicarelli for their continued interest, support, love, friendship and words of encouragement throughout my times of writing this book. They have been a true source of inspiration to keep me focused, passionate and motivated. I would like to thank Pastor Mike Housholder for his words of wisdom, which helped me as I was writing this book.

ABOUT THE AUTHOR

Ian J. Keeney is an award-winning author known for *A Thousand Pieces* and *A Better Tomorrow* as well as several short stories and poems. In addition to writing, he is also an award-winning filmmaker and musician. He has completed four feature films and several short films. He started playing drums when he was 12-years-old, plays guitar and writes music. His music is released with the band *Wolves in Clothing*.

www.ingramcontent.com/pod-product-compliance
Lightning Source LLC
Chambersburg PA
CBHW020946180626
46814CB00003B/950